SADIE'S BA

Ballerinas

Sadie's Ballet School Dream
Luci in the Spotlight

BALLERINAS

Sadie's Ballet School Dream

Harriet Castor

a division of Hodder Headline plc

First published in Great Britain in 1996
by Hodder Children's Books

10 9 8 7 6 5 4 3 2 1

A Catalogue record for this book is available from
the British Library

ISBN 0 340 65129 6

Typeset by Avon Dataset Ltd, Bidford-on-Avon, Warks

Printed and bound in Great Britain by
Cox & Wyman, Reading, Berks

Hodder and Stoughton
a division of Hodder Headline plc
338 Euston Road
London NW1 3BH

For my ballet teachers,
Beryl Thomas and Betty Pattison.
And for my parents – who, many hundreds of times, waited in the cold for the class to end.

Part One

Beginning

One

'Don't you know anything?'

Belinda flicked her hair over her shoulder and shot me a sharp, pitying look.

I felt a bit crushed by that. There are lots of things I know about – guinea pigs, for example. And long division. And Ice-Cream Crunchy (my own recipe; Mum calls it Terrible Tooth Rot). But it was true; when it came to ballet, compared to Belinda, I didn't know anything.

'The Evanova School,' said Belinda importantly, tapping the brochure with her little pink finger, 'is the best ballet school in the whole world.'

'Wow.' I stared at the picture on the front cover. There were three girls, all standing in the same position one behind the other. I knew from the *Beginning Ballet* book I'd got out of the library that the position was called an *arabesque*. The girl at the front, the smallest one, looked about my age. I stared at her in her dark blue leotard, with her hair in two plaits folded neatly over her head. I would have given anything in the world to be that girl.

'This is what the school looks like.' Belinda opened the brochure and found another photograph. It showed a grand red-brick building, with a tower over the front doorway. 'It has three acres of gardens. And six different dancing studios. There are ballet lessons all day – no maths or history or anything. And all the pupils have to board.'

'What does that mean?'

Belinda gave me another withering look. 'It means you can't go home at night, silly,' she said. 'You can only go home in the holidays.' I must have turned a bit pale, because she laughed and said, '*I* wouldn't mind. You have to be ready to give up anything to be a ballerina, or else it means you don't really want to. Lily Dempsey said so on TV.'

Lily Dempsey was Belinda's favourite dancer. She danced at Covent Garden, and had her picture on posters all over the London Underground. I remembered seeing one of them that day we went to the Science Museum. It showed Lily Dempsey soaring through the air in a *grand jeté*; and the picture had looked so beautiful I'd almost forgotten to get on the train. Belinda said Lily Dempsey had trained at this Evanova School.

'I'd give up anything,' I said suddenly.

'*You*?' Belinda raised her eyebrows. 'But I thought you said you didn't go to ballet lessons?'

'I don't,' I admitted. 'But I'm going to be a dancer one day, even so.'

To my alarm, Belinda squealed with laughter. 'No chance! You can't possibly be a ballet dancer if you haven't started lessons by *now*.'

I frowned. I was ten last birthday. Was that too late?

'I started when I was *three*,' said Belinda proudly, as if she'd read my thoughts. 'And I've been having two classes a week for the past year. But it's still not enough. That's why I'm going to audition for the Evanova School. If you want to be a dancer, you have to train full-time.'

She looked at me matter-of-factly. 'So I'll be a dancer when I grow up and you'll just have to be something else.'

But there was nothing else I wanted to be. Nothing else in the whole world.

Belinda's not really a friend of mine. Mum met Mrs Whitehead – Belinda's mother – two weeks ago at the old people's home where she's started helping out on Fridays. Mrs Whitehead was visiting her father, who lives there. Anyway, the two of them got chatting, and soon discovered they both had ten-year-old daughters. That's when they decided we should have tea together after school one day. It's funny how grown-ups think that just because you're the same age you're going to get on. They fixed the tea for this Wednesday afternoon.

Belinda wasn't at the same school as me – she went to the private girls' school on Ansty Lane, whereas I was at Middleton Combined – but our houses weren't far apart and Mum walked me round to Belinda's as soon as I got home from school.

Belinda's house was big; three storeys high, and white with squiggly bits of decoration like a giant's wedding cake. On the ground floor there was a huge bay window, and I could see through the glass that the curtains were the posh sort you tie back in the middle. We don't have curtains like that at home.

I didn't want to go in, but Mum pulled me up the stone steps and rang the bell jauntily. There were footsteps inside, and then the door swung open.

'Hello Jill!' said a woman with a big toothy smile. She looked down at me. 'You must be Sadie.'

I nodded shyly. Mrs Whitehead had a hairstyle a bit like the Queen's, but blonde. Her blouse was all blue and white stripes and the collar was turned up. She had a pearl necklace on, too. She put out a hand to me, so I shook it and said 'Nice to meet you'. I didn't think it *was* terribly nice, but I knew Mum would be cross if I didn't say it – which was funny when I thought about it, because Mum says telling lies is wrong.

'Come in, come in,' said Mrs Whitehead, standing back so we could get past into the house. But Mum was in a hurry.

'Can't stop, Audrey. I want to go up to the garden

centre before it shuts. I'll be back at half past six. Is that OK?'

'Super!' said Mrs Whitehead.

So I had to go in on my own.

The hallway had a shiny wooden floor, and a big mirror on one wall with a fancy gold frame. I was so busy trying to decide whether the round things on it were meant to be cherries or grapes, that at first I didn't notice the girl standing at the top of the stairs. And when a high voice said, 'I'm Belinda, but my middle name's Arabella. What's yours?', I almost jumped out of my skin.

'Go straight on up, Sadie,' said Mrs Whitehead, putting a hand on my back and giving me a little push towards the stairs. 'I'm sure you'd like to see Belinda's bedroom, wouldn't you?'

I climbed slowly. Belinda stayed where she was, hanging on to the banisters and staring at me. Her hair was blonde just like Mrs Whitehead's, but it hung in long curly strands down past her shoulders. She had what looked like a party dress on, and ankle socks with frills round the edges. I suddenly felt very dowdy in my jeans and Cuddle Bear sweatshirt. From the look on her face, I could tell Belinda thought so too.

'Well?' she said sharply when I reached the top step.

I looked blank. 'What's your middle name?' she repeated.

'Oh, I don't have one,' I said. 'I'm just Sadie Marsh. Dad says it took so long for him and Mum to agree on my first name that they couldn't face choosing a second.'

I smiled a little, but Belinda didn't smile back. She looked at me like I was a curiosity in a museum. 'Poor you,' she said. 'Come on, then, I'll show you my bedroom.'

We had to go up another two flights to get there, and Belinda chattered all the way about how her room had just been redecorated, and how she'd chosen the paint herself – and the carpet, and the bedclothes, and even the lampshades. At last we reached a door with a little china plaque on it which said 'Belinda' in curly letters. She opened it, and stood back to let me see, with a 'What do you think of *that*?' look on her face.

I was stunned. She must have thought I was really impressed, because she smiled a smug smile and said, 'Daddy says it cost an *awful* lot of money.'

I didn't say a word; I just stared. Everything – and I mean *everything* – was pink. The walls were pink. The ceiling was pink. The carpet was dark pink, with pale pink flecks in it. The duvet cover was pink with a white frill round it and pillows to match. Even the wardrobe was pink, with little pink fancy handles. No prizes for guessing *her* favourite colour, Dad would have said.

I do quite like pink – but this was like living in a candyfloss castle. I was just wondering whether I should be polite and say how lovely it was, when I spotted something over on the far side of the room.

I stared; and my mouth dropped open in amazement.

It was hanging up on one of the wardrobe doors. Part of it was made of something silky, which caught the light in shimmering folds. Then, below that, there were layers and layers of net sticking stiffly out at the sides. A few months ago, I wouldn't have known the proper name for it. But I did now: it was a tutu.

I ran over to where it hung, and gingerly felt the material.

'Don't touch!' Belinda snapped, following me and snatching it away. 'It's my best one. Mummy only bought it yesterday.'

'It's your very own?' I asked in awe, trying to imagine what it felt like to have a real tutu. 'Do you wear it?'

'Of course,' said Belinda. She held it up against herself and looked in the mirror admiringly. 'Only for shows, though. For normal lessons Miss Cole makes us wear boring old leotards.'

To me, proper ballet leotards sounded anything but boring, but I knew Belinda would think me silly if I said so.

'Is Miss Cole your dancing teacher?' I asked.

'Yes,' said Belinda. 'She's quite good, Mummy says. Who's yours?'

'I don't have one,' I admitted, and felt my cheeks flush.

Belinda gave me a curious look, as if she thought only martians didn't have ballet teachers.

'Why ever not?' she asked.

When I explained that Mum wouldn't let me go to dancing lessons, Belinda said, 'How perfectly beastly.'

I thought it was beastly too, but I didn't like someone else saying that about Mum, so I said, 'It's because I have piano lessons, actually, and we can't afford both.'

'Gosh,' said Belinda, looking surprised. 'You must be terribly poor. I have piano lessons as well as ballet – and elocution and singing and extra French, too. My French teacher's called Mademoiselle Simone. She's ever so pretty.'

I didn't care a bit what Mademoiselle Simone looked like, and I felt cross with Belinda for thinking we were so badly off. But then she got out the Evanova School brochure and began to tell me about it, and soon I couldn't be cross any more; I was too busy worrying whether it was really too late for me to start training, like Belinda said.

Then Belinda opened her wardrobe and showed me another tutu – she called it a 'horrid old thing'. She showed me her leotards, too – six of them, all in different shades of pink – and her pink satin ballet shoes with their long trailing ribbons.

I picked up the shoes in wonder; I'd seen ballet shoes in pictures, of course, and in the window of the Dancewear shop on Smith Street, but I'd never touched a real pair before. The satin was so smooth and shiny; I rubbed it against my cheek.

'Can I try them on?' I asked.

'No.' Belinda took them back. 'Your feet are far

too big – you'll stretch them.' I glanced down; my feet looked exactly the same size as hers.

Belinda pulled at my sleeve. 'But look – I'll show you how I tie the ribbons.' And she slipped off her sandals and put the ballet shoes on, criss-crossing the ribbons over her ankles and tying them in a little knot at the side.

Then she did some steps for me.

'This one's called a *pas de chat*,' she said, springing in the air and bending up each leg in turn. 'It means "step of the cat".'

Next, she pawed the ground with one pointed foot.

'And this one's a *pas de cheval*,' she explained. 'Which means "step of the horse".'

Much as I wanted not to, I couldn't help feeling impressed.

'Tea's ready.' Mrs Whitehead popped her head round the door, just as Belinda was doing a party polka round the room, her blonde curls bouncing as she went. 'Oh, Belinda!' said Mrs Whitehead. 'How nice to see you practising! You know, Sadie, it must be the first time she's practised in months.'

I stared at Belinda in amazement. With tutus and satin shoes to dress up in, how could she bear not to dance all the time?

Belinda looked at me defiantly when her mother had gone. 'Miss Cole thinks I'm the best in the class,' she said proudly. 'So why should I need to practise?'

I wondered what Lily Dempsey would have said about *that*.

Two

I haven't always been mad on ballet. A year ago I was desperate to have a pony, only Mum said we couldn't afford one and Dad said we'd have nowhere to put it, as our back garden's ever so small. Then after that, I saw a Young Musician competition on TV and suddenly I wanted to play the piano. We've got an old one in the sitting-room, so a man came and tuned it for me to practise on, and I started going to Mrs Winter's house for lessons every Thursday.

I liked Mrs Winter a lot, but I soon found out I didn't like piano. All those boring scales and fiddly finger exercises – it wasn't anything like as fun as I'd expected!

So when I discovered that what I really wanted to do was ballet, I thought there'd be no problem swapping piano lessons for ballet lessons. But it wasn't as simple as that.

I found out about ballet on my tenth birthday. Dad took me to the cinema to see a film called *The Red Shoes*. He said he'd first seen it when he was little, so I thought it was going to be one of those really boring films in black and white like they have on TV on Saturday afternoons. But I was wrong; it was the most brilliant film I'd ever seen.

It was about a ballet dancer, and the main part

was played by a woman called Moira Shearer. She was as pale as milk, just like me, but while I've got mousy brown hair, hers was a bright, glowing red. It hung down her neck and looked beautiful against her white ballet dress. The best thing of all, though, was her dancing – I'd never seen anything like it. Spinning on the tips of her toes, balancing, jumping as if it was just as easy to be in the air as on the ground – she was glorious!

The film's story was a sad one – I won't give it away in case you haven't seen it yet – and by the end there were lots of sniffles coming from all round the cinema. I even saw Dad dab at the corners of his eyes with a hanky he keeps tucked up the sleeve of his jumper. But I didn't cry; I felt happy. I'd just discovered exactly what I wanted to be.

And from that moment on, all I could think about was ballet.

As soon as I got home I pleaded with Mum and Dad to let me start lessons. Dad seemed to think it was quite a good idea, but Mum put her foot down.

'You've only just started piano. We can't pay for something else as well.'

'I'll give up piano, then!' I said, trying a lopsided Moira Shearer spin which made my plaits fly out like helicopter wings.

'Sadie Marsh, you never stick at anything!' said Mum. 'Last week piano, this week ballet. What will it be next week? Gymnastics?'

'Mud-wrestling? Potholing? Astronomy?' This was

Dad talking now, as he crashed about in the sink, looking for a clean mug for his tea. 'Try them all, Tiger, then you'll be a whizz on *The Golden Ticket*!'

The Golden Ticket is Dad's favourite quiz show. It's on every week day and he has to shut himself in his study to watch it because Mum doesn't approve.

'Simon,' said Mum sharply. 'I'm being serious here. Sadie asked for piano lessons and that's what she's got. End of story.'

And it looked like it was. However much I pleaded and nagged, Mum wouldn't let me start ballet. I even tried offering to do lots of jobs around the house to make her change her mind.

'I'll make my bed every day!'

'You should be doing that anyway.'

'I'll do all the washing-up for a week.'

'No.'

'I'll do the gardening, then.'

'Look, Sadie, how many times do I have to say it? No, no, no!'

It was useless. Mum was probably hoping I'd forget about ballet soon enough. But I didn't.

I went to the library, and took out as many books on ballet as I could find. Books on its history, with pictures of the French king Louis XIV and drawings of women a hundred years ago with white floaty skirts and tiny tiny feet. Story books about girls who went to ballet school and became famous dancers. I got books out on ballet technique, too, and I copied the pictures, learning the five positions of the feet and the special French words for things, like *plié, tendu* and *arabesque*. I began to practise every night, wearing my swimming costume instead of a leotard and holding on to the radiator in my bedroom for a barre. Sometimes I practised in front of the bathroom mirror. I don't think I looked much like Moira Shearer, though.

And every night, when I put the light out in my little attic bedroom, I dreamt of having dancing lessons. Of putting on ballet shoes, with their beautiful satin ribbons, and a white floaty skirt like Moira Shearer's and, one day, of dancing on a real stage. Even though Mum wouldn't let me go to classes, I knew I was going to be a ballerina – somehow.

Until, that is, Belinda Whitehead said to me, 'You can't possibly be a ballet dancer if you haven't started lessons by *now* . . .' It felt as if an ice cube had been dropped down my back. Too late to train to be a dancer? I shivered at the thought.

That night, I searched through all the ballet books on my shelf, but I couldn't find a single ballerina who'd learnt just by practising at home. One thing was clear: whatever Mum said, I had to join a ballet class – there was no time to lose. But how was I going to do it?

Three

'You all right, Tiger?' Dad peered at me blearily. He'd lost his glasses – again – and he's blind as a bat without them. He loses them every morning.

'Fine,' I said through a mouthful of crumbs.

'Sadie.' Mum frowned at me. She's very hot on table manners.

I chewed and chewed and then swallowed. 'Sorry,' I said.

I wasn't fine actually. I'd been awake half the night trying to think up a new plan for persuading Mum to let me start ballet, but I hadn't got anywhere.

'Sorrysorrysorrysorry,' repeated Thomas in a singsong voice, patting Oliver rather hard on the head with a very sticky hand. 'Waagghh!' said Oliver. Mum sighed. She was looking hassled.

My brothers, Thomas and Oliver – or Squit and Squirt as Dad calls them – are both two years old. They're twins. Sometimes – just sometimes – they can be very sweet, like when they snuggle up to you on the sofa and suck their thumbs and fall asleep. But mostly they're a complete pain, and these days Mum always looks tired. They never seem to get to Dad in the same way. Mind you, Dad would look relaxed if the house was falling down around his ears.

'Simon.' Mum was looking at her watch. 'Sadie's got to go in ten minutes.'

'Right-ho.' Dad stuck a piece of toast between his teeth and stood up. He was still in his stripy nightshirt – he always wears it to breakfast, even on work days: his long stripy nightshirt and his socks.

'Crumbs!' Mum pointed to the toast in his mouth. Dad looked apologetic and held a hand under his chin as he padded out into the hallway and started wearily up the stairs.

Ten minutes later we were in the car.

'Clunk-click,' said Dad to himself as he put his seat belt on. I was already strapped in, in the front passenger seat.

'Dad?'

'Yes, Tiger?'

For a split second I thought of telling him everything Belinda had said and asking him what I should do. But then I changed my mind. If Mum and Dad ever disagreed about anything, Mum always won. Getting Dad to say yes to things was easy – and nearly always useless.

'Something bothering you?' Dad flicked the indicator off as the car juddered on to the road.

'Doesn't matter,' I mumbled. I frowned at the houses and shop fronts as they whizzed by. Loads of people went to ballet lessons. Their mothers let them. Why couldn't mine? It just wasn't fair.

When I got to school it had started raining, and everyone was in the form room. My best friend

Robbie (her real name's Roberta, but you mustn't call her that because she hates it) has the desk next to me, and she was busy laying out her equipment in neat rows: pencils, pens, rubbers, rulers – she always has at least three of everything. I don't know how she finds room on her desk for her exercise book.

'The trouble is,' said Robbie when I told her my problem, 'you've either got to convince your mum that you're really serious about ballet . . .'

'Or?' I said, because I'd tried that already and it hadn't worked.

Robbie sucked her pencil for a moment, scrunching her nose to stop her glasses slipping down. 'Or – you've got to find the money so that you can go to ballet lessons as well as piano.'

Robbie's really brainy. She wants to be a history professor when she grows up. Don't ask me why – compared to ballet I think even the best stories about kings and queens are really boring.

'But I only get 50p pocket money a week,' I said glumly.

'How much are ballet lessons?' Robbie rummaged in her satchel for her calculator.

'Not sure,' I said. 'A lot more than 50p.'

'Oh.' Robbie frowned. Then she had another idea. 'I know! You could have an accident which means you can't play the piano – then you'll *have* to give it up!' She seemed really pleased with that one.

'What sort of accident?'

'I don't know – break your fingers or something.'

'Ouch!' I said, feeling sick just thinking about it. 'But dancers have to have nice hands. It says so in my book.'

'Oh.' Robbie frowned again.

Then Mrs Turner came in to take the register, so we had to stop talking. I sighed. It seemed hopeless.

Plonk, plonk, *plunk*.

'Oh bother!'

I'd forgotten the F sharp again and the chord sounded horrid. Mrs Winter narrowed her eyes.

'Sadie,' she said crisply. 'How many concert pianists do you know who end a performance with a cry of "Oh bother"?'

'Sorry, Mrs Winter.'

'I don't want sorry!' Mrs Winter sighed dramatically. 'I want fire! I want enthusiasm! I want F sharps in the right places!'

Mrs Winter is one of my favourite people in the world. She looks about a hundred, has skin like a dried-up prune, a voice like a foghorn, and the most amazing collection of hats you have ever seen. She must have hundreds, because I don't think I've spotted her in the same one twice.

Today she was wearing a large straw one, with a bunch of shiny cherries on its brim.

'Your heart's not in this, is it, my dear?' she boomed.

It was no use lying to Mrs Winter. She could always tell.

'No,' I admitted in a small voice. I didn't want to

hurt her feelings, though, so I added hurriedly, 'But I did want to play the piano – when I started, I mean. It's just that Mum says we can only afford one sort of lessons at a time, and . . . well . . . there's something else I want to do more.'

'I see,' said Mrs Winter. 'And what is this something else, pray?'

'Ballet,' I whispered, looking down at the piano keys.

'Ah!' said Mrs Winter, so loudly it made me jump. 'You want to be a dancer?'

I nodded fervently. 'More than anything else in the world!'

'But your mother will not let you give up lessons with me in order to learn?'

'No.' I was rather shamefaced. 'She says I'm always changing my mind, and that I never stick at anything.' I looked up eagerly. 'But that's only because, before, I hadn't found out what I really wanted to do! It must have been ballet all along, only I didn't know it!'

'I see,' said Mrs Winter, reaching for the butter-scotch tin. 'Here, dear. Take one.' I picked out a sweet and unwrapped the little square of gold paper carefully.

Mrs Winter seemed to be thinking. She reached for a butterscotch herself and took an age unwrapping it. Then she popped it in her mouth and sucked on it slowly.

'It is a terrible thing,' she said at last, 'to know your heart's desire and yet to be denied it.' There was a dreamy look in her eyes for a moment. Then she looked at me suddenly. 'But, my dear, ballet is a cruel art. A great art, yes, but a cruel one. Even the most talented dancer lives every day with pain and suffering. And the work never ends until the moment you retire. Are you prepared for that?'

I had read in my library books about the determination needed to be a dancer. Anyone, they said, who thought ballet was all bouquets of flowers and pretty dresses would never work hard enough to succeed. I'd promised myself I wouldn't make that mistake. 'I'd spend every minute practising if I could,' I said eagerly, 'just like they do at the Evanova School.'

'The Evanova?' Mrs Winter looked at me sharply.

'It's the best ballet school in the world, Belinda says,' I explained. 'They have ballet lessons all day – no maths, or history, or anything. And all the pupils have to board.'

'Fiddlesticks!' said Mrs Winter suddenly, scowling at me.

'They do!' I protested. 'It means they can only go home in the holidays.'

'Yes, yes, I wasn't referring to the matter of boarding.' She flapped a hand in the air. 'This no maths or history business. That is quite, quite wrong. Pupils at the Evanova School spend as much time on academic studies as you do, Sadie. It is very important to get a good education.'

'But Belinda–'

'Belinda – whoever she may be – clearly has her head full of cotton-wool.'

'Hrrmmph.' That was the sound of me squashing down a giggle. Mrs Winter says I have a silly giggle, so I try not to do it in front of her. But the thought of haughty Belinda with a big fluffy cloud of cotton-wool where her head should be was too much for me – I began to laugh.

'Enough, enough!' Mrs Winter clapped her hands briskly. 'I see we have overrun the allotted lesson time yet again. You must go, my dear.'

Still gulping with laughter, I slid off the piano-stool and ran to fetch my coat. A moment later, we were standing in the shadowy hallway. Mrs Winter looked at me searchingly.

'Sadie.' She bent down so that her face was level with mine. It smelt of butterscotch and talcum powder. 'If you really mean what you say about wanting to dance, then perhaps there is something we can do about it. I shall ponder the matter. But –' she held up a wrinkled finger sternly, '– you must think too, my dear. Very carefully. I want you to be quite sure that there is nothing else – nothing else in the world – that you wish to do with your life.'

'But there isn't–'

'Don't tell me now,' Mrs Winter interrupted. 'Go home and consider. We shall have another chat next week.' And with that, she ushered me out of the door.

It was only much later, when I was in my bedroom practising my *pliés*, that I thought back over everything she had said – about being dedicated and about the Evanova School, too. And suddenly it struck me: for a piano teacher, Mrs Winter seemed to know an awful lot about ballet.

Four

'What's the capital of Switzerland?' said Dad, pointing at me.

'Bern!' I shouted, pressing an imaginary buzzer on the table. I only knew it because we'd had that one yesterday, and Dad had had to tell me the answer.

'Very good, Contestant One,' said Dad. 'Contestants Two and Three,' he turned to the twins, 'have been disqualified for answering no questions at all, and for putting jam sandwiches on their heads.' Thomas and Oliver clapped their sticky hands together. They didn't seem to mind being disqualified.

'That means that you, Contestant One,' Dad turned to me again, 'will go through to the grand final and have a chance to win . . .'

'The Golden Ticket!' we chorused together.

'Oh blimey.' Mum appeared in the doorway.

'Contestant Four, you are a very late entry,' said Dad severely. 'But here on *The Golden Ticket* everyone has the chance to be a winner. So – can you . . . name the longest river in the world?'

Mum ignored him. She put the car keys on the table and took her coat off. 'I'll have to hurry you,' said Dad, pretending the pepper grinder was a stopwatch. 'Time's up! Contestant One?'

'The Nile!' I shouted triumphantly.

Today I was excited, though not because of Dad's quiz. The week since my piano lesson had passed really slowly, but now at last Thursday had come round again. I couldn't wait to find out if Mrs Winter had any ideas about how I could start ballet.

'I'm off to piano!' I sang, skipping out of the kitchen to go and find my sheet music. Feeling grateful in advance for Mrs Winter's help, I'd even done more practice than usual.

'Have fun, love!' called Mum.

'See you, see you, see you!' I called back, and slammed the door behind me.

It was a grey December day, and a strong east wind was blowing the last few autumn leaves along the pavement. I pulled my duffle coat round me and felt in the pockets for my mittens.

Mrs Winter only lives two streets away from us – even nearer than Belinda, but in the opposite direction. On Belinda's street all the houses are massive, but on Mrs Winter's they're more like ours; narrow-fronted, with one window downstairs and two upstairs.

Mrs Winter's house was number fifteen. Three cracked and mossy stone steps led up to the dark blue front door. High up on the door, just below the brass 1 and 5, there was a knocker in the shape of a wiggly fish, tail up. I liked that knocker, but I'd never used it; now, as always, I stretched up my hand to push the bell button instead.

A tuneless buzz sounded somewhere deep inside. A few seconds later the door-lock clunked and Mrs Winter appeared. She was wearing a long shapeless dress, the same gravy colour as the wallpaper behind her. But on her head was something very special. If you hadn't known it was a hat, you might have thought that it was a strange bird crouching there, because all you could see were feathers. They were tiny thin ones, and they swayed gently back and forth every time she moved her head.

'Ah, Sadie. How nice to see you,' said Mrs Winter, just as she always did. 'Do come in.'

I was expecting that we would chat straight away, and when I had taken off my coat and sat down on the piano-stool, I hesitated to get out my music. But Mrs Winter said, 'Let's have some scales, shall we? C major first.'

And when, after the scales, Mrs Winter chose one of my pieces – and then another, I began to wonder whether she'd forgotten altogether. I soldiered on, feeling more and more miserable with every note I played.

'Much better this week,' declared Mrs Winter at last. ' "Fifes and Drums" is quite pleasing now, my dear. I don't think it would be a good idea for you to give up piano lessons, you know.'

I looked at her quickly; she hadn't forgotten after all. But did this mean she wouldn't help me?

'I have thought, like you told me to, Mrs Winter, and I'm absolutely sure . . .' My voice trailed away.

Mrs Winter blinked slowly. 'After all,' she said, as if I hadn't spoken, 'musicality is an extremely important quality in a dancer. Sit over there, my dear –' she gestured to a threadbare armchair in the corner '– and I will fetch some lemonade.'

A moment later Mrs Winter returned. She set down a wooden tray, and handed me a tall glass full of cloudy lemonade. I sipped it carefully; it didn't taste as I expected – it was sharper, like real lemon juice. But, after another sip, I decided I liked it.

'I am not as mobile as I once was,' said Mrs Winter, settling back in her chair with a waft of feathers. 'My knees and my back are giving me trouble and I don't find housework as easy as I used to. Are you a church-goer?'

The question startled me; I couldn't see what this had to do with ballet lessons. 'Erm . . .' I hesitated. 'We went last Christmas. And Auntie Geraldine got married in June – that was in a church.'

'An occasional church-goer!' boomed Mrs Winter. 'The very worst sort – neither one thing nor the other. I presume your Sunday mornings are free, then?'

'Well, sometimes we go swimming–'

'Good,' said Mrs Winter as if swimming didn't count. 'If your mother agrees – and I say *if*, Sadie; you must ask her and she may say no – you will come to me on Sunday mornings, starting next week. You will help me with the housework – clearing out cupboards, dusting, that sort of thing – and perhaps, when the spring comes, you will help me in the garden too. This, in turn, will help you.'

I was thoroughly confused. 'How come?'

'Not "how come?", Sadie. Try "why is that?", instead.'

'Why is that, Mrs Winter?'

'Because, my dear, for your help on Sunday mornings I shall be prepared to pay you the princely sum of three pounds a week. Now,' she held up a hand as I opened my mouth to speak, 'I am aware that three pounds may not be enough, but I imagine that you have a little pocket money of your own that you may be able to add to it. And also, if I am not very much mistaken, girls of your age are sometimes given money for Christmas by unimaginative relatives, are they not?'

I nodded.

'So,' Mrs Winter looked satisfied. 'Altogether, this may go some way towards paying for you to have ballet lessons. I say *may*, my dear,' she added, with emphasis, 'you must ask your mother what she thinks.'

A flash of regret suddenly shot through my mind as I thought of what I'd been hoping to buy with my Christmas money: a soda fountain, perhaps, or a new school bag. But, in an instant, the thought was gone. How could I possibly think of soda fountains or bags when I could have ballet lessons instead?

'Oh, thank you, Mrs Winter!' I said. 'It's a wonderful idea! And I shan't mind missing swimming if it means I can learn ballet!'

'You may find, my dear,' said Mrs Winter wisely, 'that swimming is just the first of many things you will have to sacrifice if you really want to dance.'

Mum wouldn't say no – I was determined.

When I got home, she was in the bathroom washing her hair. I went straight up and sat next to her on the bathroom chair. It's blue wicker and it drops bits on the carpet.

'Mum . . .' Suddenly I didn't quite know how to begin. 'Mrs Winter's had an idea . . .'

I told Mum the whole story; how I'd talked to Mrs Winter about ballet the week before and then she'd thought about it, and then we'd had lemonade and she'd come up with her plan. Every so often Mum had to say, 'Pardon?' and 'What did you say?' because the water got into her ears.

By the time I'd finished, she was wringing out her hair. It's quite long and it hung down into the basin like a thick slippery snake.

'Sadie – I do wish you hadn't gone telling strangers what we can and can't afford.' Mum was frowning.

'But she isn't a stranger! She's Mrs Winter!'

'You know what I mean.' She reached for a towel, put it over her hair, and twisted it up into a turban. 'And it wasn't very polite of you to say that you didn't like her lessons, was it?'

I blushed. 'I suppose not,' I admitted. 'But Mum – she didn't seem to mind. And I'm not going to stop piano anyway. She said that learning music is very good for dancers.'

'Sounds like a bit of a know-all, this Mrs Winter character,' said Dad, looking in on his way past. 'Bet she'd be good on *The Golden Ti–*'

'So you see I'm sticking at piano, like you wanted,' I went on. 'And with the money I'll earn from Mrs Winter, and my pocket money and my Christmas money–'

'*If* you get any,' Mum said. Then, to my surprise, she laughed. 'Well, it's certainly a good test of your dedication! I'll be impressed if you last five minutes with no spending money.'

Did she mean . . . ? I looked at her eagerly, and Mum saw the question in my face. 'All right, Sadie,' she said at last. 'Let's give it a try.'

I could hardly believe my ears. 'How soon can I start lessons?'

'After Christmas. You're going to use your Christmas money, remember? And stop bouncing up and down – you're making me feel queasy.'

Christmas was two and a half weeks away – I wanted to start *tomorrow*. But still I was delighted.

'Oh thank you, thank you, thank you, Mum,' I said happily.

And thank you Mrs Winter, I added in my head.

Five

I've never known a Christmas go so fast. Usually I long for it to linger – I try and stay up as late as possible on Christmas night, just to stop it being over, and I wake up on Boxing Day feeling terribly flat, knowing that it won't be Christmas again for another 365 long, long days.

But this year, I didn't care at all when Christmas tripped by. I even went to bed early on Christmas night. I *wanted* it to be gone, because then it would be January – and on Saturday 6th January, at ten thirty a.m., I was to have my first ballet lesson.

On the Wednesday before, Mum took me to the sales to buy my ballet equipment. I'd stared through the window of Dancewear many times, but this was my first trip inside.

It was amazing. The walls were a honeycomb of cubbyholes, and in each hole there was a stack of ballet shoes, all squashed flat on top of one another, like pitta breads. Above one section, a small label said 'Pointe Shoes' – and the shop assistant pulled some out for me to look at. I was shocked at how hard the toe-ends were – Mum said you could have banged a nail into a wall with them!

'You won't be needing a pair of these for a good while, I'd imagine,' said the shop assistant, smiling gently and holding out her hands for the shoes.

I was reluctant to give them back – I wanted to take them home and try out standing on my toes – 'on pointes', the books called it. But I knew I shouldn't; I knew that it was dangerous, and that girls who danced on pointes before their muscles were strong enough and their bones were properly hardened could ruin their chances of ever becoming ballerinas. I passed the shoes to the assistant with a small sigh.

There weren't just ballet shoes in the shop, of course, there were clothes too – racks of leotards, gauzy skirts and tunics. There were even a few tutus, just like Belinda's.

I could have spent all day there, trying everything on. But Mum was firm; I had to choose one leotard – and it had to be from the Sale rack. In the end, I found there was only one that was just the right size – and, to my disappointment, it was green, my least favourite colour.

I didn't get the shoes I'd hoped for, either. Instead of satin ones, Mum insisted I should have leather, and instead of ribbons to cross over my ankles, she bought two short pieces of elastic.

'But Mum,' I pleaded, 'everyone else in the class is bound to have pink satins.'

'Nonsense,' said Mum. 'I checked with the teacher. She recommended the leather shoes as they're more hard-wearing.'

So that was that. And, with a pair of pink ballet tights chosen and a pink headband too, we were soon out of the shop. I had never imagined I could come back from Dancewear feeling disappointed – but I did, just a little.

Nothing, however, could dampen my excitement when Saturday morning finally came. I woke up at seven o'clock, and though there was bags of time to spare, I felt far too jittery to lie in bed a minute longer.

When Dad came downstairs at eight I was already washing up my cereal bowl. I was dressed too, with my tights and leotard on underneath the leggings and matching sweatshirt Auntie Geraldine had given me for Christmas.

'Ready already, Twinkletoes?' said Dad, rubbing his eyes. 'What have you got planned for the next couple of hours? Fancy giving Squit and Squirt their breakfast?'

'No fear!' I laughed.

I ran upstairs and put my pink leather ballet shoes on. I made sure the drawstrings round the edges were tied exactly right – not so tight that they cut into my heels at the back, but not so loose, either, that the leather gaped at the sides. When each drawstring was fastened in a tiny bow, I tucked the ends out of sight. Then I tried out some *pliés*, and some *battements tendus*, and some *ronds de jambe à terre* tracing my toe in a semi-circle on the floor first *en dehors* – outwardly – and then *en dedans* – inwardly – though it's terribly easy to confuse the two!

And it was still only half past eight. I pulled down my leggings and checked for the umpteenth time that the seams on the back of my ballet tights were straight. Then I checked that all my hair things were ready for when Mum got up: elastics, grips, pins, hairnet. I got out one of my library books too, to show her what I wanted: two plaits, folded over the top of my head, just like that girl on the front of the Evanova School brochure.

Mum had more trouble with the hairstyle than I expected. I've been growing my hair for ages – I can just about sit on it when it's loose – and the two plaits were so long that they folded right over my head and the ends hung down beside my ears. Mum had to put in every single pin and grip we had to curl them back and hold them in place.

But when it was finished, I felt like a real ballet dancer.

'Careful when you take your sweatshirt off,' warned Mum. 'I don't want to have to do it all again.'

And at last it was time to go. Mum had arranged for me to start lessons with Miss Cole, the same teacher Belinda went to. She taught at the community centre, which was only five minutes' drive away.

I got into the car feeling like a queen, and tried to sit with my back straight and my neck long and elegant all the way there. But when the car drew up in the community centre carpark and Mum clicked off the engine, I started to feel a bit nervous. I sat there for a minute, quite still, until Mum said, 'Out you get, then.'

Inside the community centre you come to a little hallway first, which Miss Cole's pupils use as a waiting room. It's rather drafty, and I noticed that most of the children had done the same as me, and changed into their ballet clothes at home. Then, with a sting of surprise, I spotted Belinda over in the corner, waiting with her mother. She had a pink hairband on and her blonde hair was done up in a bun.

'Oh, look, there's Audrey Whitehead and Belinda,' said Mum.

I hoped we wouldn't have to go and talk to them, but Mum waved, and then there was no option.

'Good to see you, Jill,' said Mrs Whitehead. 'I didn't know Sadie came to ballet.'

'First time,' said Mum.

'Oh super!' said Mrs Whitehead.

'You can't be in my class,' Belinda whispered to me. 'You belong with the babies. You must have got the time wrong.'

I pulled on Mum's sleeve. 'I don't know, Sadie,' she said when I asked her. 'But I'm sure Miss Cole said ten thirty – I remember it clearly.'

The little hallway had a door through into the big room where Miss Cole taught her classes. I knew what the room looked like – I'd been to a Brownies' show there once which Robbie was in. The room was large, with a stage at one end, and thick red curtains you could draw across the front of it like a real theatre. There was a piano, too, and lots of chairs that got stacked by the walls when they weren't needed.

Now I heard voices wafting through the doorway. They were chanting, 'Thank you, Miss Cole. Thank you, Mr Arthur.'

'They're doing their curtsies,' said Belinda knowledgeably. 'Mr Arthur is the pianist. You have to curtsey to him too, to say thank you for playing for the class.'

'Oh,' I said, wondering whether I would remember, and whether Mr Arthur would be offended if I didn't. There seemed so many things that you had to do just right in ballet.

That moment the door to the big hall swung open and about twenty-five older girls and boys rushed out, all red in the face – they must have been jumping up and down a lot.

It was time for our class to go in. Belinda pushed forward, dragging her mother with her, and Mum and I followed.

The other children put their bags down at the back of the hall, and quickly took off their cardigans and tied up the ribbons on their shoes. At the far end of the room, just in front of the stage, I saw a woman talking to a man at the piano. She was bending over some sheet music.

'That's Miss Cole,' I heard Belinda's mother say, and Mum led me off towards her.

Miss Cole looked exactly how a dancer should look – except she was a bit too old to be one, I think. She had dark brown hair, scraped into a bun. At the sides it looked like it was scraped so smoothly and tightly it must have pulled on her cheeks, but she didn't seem to mind.

'Hello, Sadie,' she said, when Mum had told her who we were. 'I thought you could join in with this class today and see how you get on.' She turned to Mum. 'It's not the beginners, Mrs Marsh. All my beginners this term are a lot younger than Sadie. I thought she'd be happier here, as the children are her own age.'

In the same class as Belinda? I gulped.

'Don't worry, Sadie,' said Miss Cole. 'I certainly won't expect you to pick up everything straight away. Just try your best.'

I ran to the back and put my bag down with the others. I got out my leather ballet shoes and took off my outdoor clothes, being careful not to spoil my hair.

'I'll pick you up in forty-five minutes,' whispered Mum, and then she was gone.

Miss Cole clapped her hands. 'To the barre, boys and girls. Feet in first position. Let's have some nice *pliés*, shall we?'

The barre was fixed to the wall along one side of the room. I found a place at the back. Belinda was four people in front of me, and seeing that I was going to join in with her class after all, she shot me an unfriendly look. I suddenly thought that coming to ballet might not have been such a good idea.

But as soon as the music began, I forgot Belinda completely. It felt odd to be resting my hand on a proper barre, rather than a radiator, and to be listening to real music, rather than just humming it in my head. But I found that I recognised a lot of the steps Miss Cole asked the class to do. Not all of them, of course, and many times I had to copy the girl in front, but I wasn't half as lost as I thought I would be. Even Miss Cole seemed pleased.

'Good, Sadie,' she said, coming up and adjusting my arm. I was holding it out in second position and she turned it a little so that my elbow didn't sag. 'Try to relax those shoulders, now.'

I nodded and tried.

Miss Cole was wonderful. She stood up very straight – standing tall, she called it when she was trying to get us to do it too – and everything she did was graceful, even when she was just walking across the room, or bending to pick something up off the floor.

She was wearing a shiny, clinging black top with long sleeves. Belinda told me afterwards it was a leotard, but you couldn't see the bottom because she had a floaty wraparound skirt on over it. Her legs were very slim, which must be an achievement when you're pretty old. She was probably about the same age as Dad. He was forty last year, and said that life begins at it but that was only to cheer himself up. I'm sure Dad's legs aren't as good as Miss Cole's. I've only seen the bottom bits of them though, because his nightshirt's very long. But his ankles are thick and hairy.

Anyway, on her legs Miss Cole was wearing pink ballet tights, and these strange soft pink shoes with tiny heels and a little T-bar. They were special shoes because I noticed she could point her feet really well in them, and most ordinary shoes are too hard for that.

As I watched her I just couldn't keep the smile off my face. Miss Cole was a real ballet teacher, and this was a real ballet class – and I was loving it.

By the time we got to *ronds de jambe à terre*, I was feeling so confident that I even put my hand up to answer a question.

'There are two sorts of *ronds de jambe*,' said Miss Cole. 'Can anyone tell me what they are called? Yes, Sadie.'

'*En dehors* and *en dedans*,' I said.

Suddenly, the whole class burst out laughing. What was so funny? I was sure I'd said the right answer – I could see the words now, on the page of *Beginning Ballet*.

Even Miss Cole was smiling. 'That's right,' she said. 'But because the words are French, we say them rather differently.'

I'd forgotten that. I'd only ever seen the words written down, and I'd said them just as they were spelt: 'en dee-horse' and 'en dee-danz'. When Miss Cole said them, though, they sounded quite different: 'on day-or' and 'on dud-on'.

The class was still giggling, and I noticed that Belinda was giggling most of all. My cheeks burnt in shame. I stared at my feet; I wanted the wooden floor to open beneath them and swallow me up. I vowed never to answer another question in class again.

When we'd finished the exercises at the barre to warm up our muscles, Miss Cole asked us to spread out in rows in the centre of the room. I stayed at the back – I felt safer there. We did a lovely *port de bras*, where you have to try and move your arms really softly and gracefully, and then we learnt a step I didn't know, called a *glissade*. It means 'gliding step', Miss Cole told us; you have to glide from one foot to the other. It's rather tricky and I could see I was going to have to practise it a good deal at home.

Then my second disaster happened. Towards the end of the class we did some *allegros* – jumping steps. As I bounced up and down, doing my *petits jetés* and my spring points, I heard a little tinkling sound. At first I wondered what it could be – and then, with horror, I realised. All my hairpins and grips were coming out one by one and dropping onto the floor at my feet. I could feel my plaits getting looser and looser. By the time we'd finished the *enchaînement*, one of my plaits was hanging down on my shoulder, while the other was still on my head. The boy next to me started laughing, and soon the ripple had spread all around the class. I wanted to run out of the room – but I didn't dare in case Miss Cole got cross. Miss Cole didn't join in with the laughter this time. 'Don't be silly, Julian,' she said sharply to the boy next to me. 'And point those feet of yours!'

In a pause between exercises, I hastily gathered up the pins and put them in my bag. As I ran back to my place I saw Belinda looking at me with a superior smile. After that, I longed for the class to end, and the minute we'd done our curtsies and said thank you to Miss Cole and Mr Arthur, I grabbed my things and raced for the door. I didn't wait for Belinda.

'Ooh, I can see we need to practise that.' Mum, who was waiting in the hallway, made a face when she saw my hair. I grabbed the plait that was still fastened on top of my head and yanked it free. Pins and grips tinkled to the floor. Why had I ever wanted to start ballet?

Suddenly I felt a hand on my shoulder. 'She did extremely well, Mrs Marsh,' said Miss Cole's voice behind me. 'Exceptionally well for a beginner. She seems very promising.' I felt a glow of pride.

'Perhaps you could try your hair in a bun next week?' Miss Cole said to me. 'And don't wash it just before you come to class – it makes it more slippery.' With that, she was gone – back into the main hall, where her next set of pupils was already waiting for her.

Part Two

One Step At a Time

Six

'So, my dear, are you working hard at your ballet?'

It was a sunny Sunday morning, and I was standing on a chair in Mrs Winter's small kitchen, washing down the windows. Mrs Winter was keeping me company at the table with a tin of polish and a collection of brass ornaments.

'Oh yes.' I paused for a minute, rubbing hard at a smeary bit. 'There! I'm awfully behind the others in my class, so I'm doing extra practice every night.'

'On your own?'

I nodded. 'I get home from school, have a drink and a biscuit, then do my homework, and then–'

'And then you do your piano practice, of course,' put in Mrs Winter.

I blushed. I didn't want to say so, but since I'd started ballet, I really hadn't been working as hard on my piano as I should.

'Go on, my dear,' laughed Mrs Winter. 'You were saying?'

'Erm . . . oh yes, after all that, I change into my ballet clothes and go through the new steps we did in last week's class. Miss Cole says you have to get each step just right on its own before you can put it with other steps and make a dance. She says it's like learning new words and then using them in a sentence.'

'That sounds very sensible to me,' said Mrs Winter. She looked at the clock. 'Ah! Time for our lemonade break!'

I enjoyed my Sunday mornings with Mrs Winter. She always asked me about my ballet, and the new things I'd learnt. Sometimes she even gave me little tips, too.

'When you do your *port de bras*,' she said one week, 'think of dragging your arms through thick treacle.'

I put down my duster and tried it out.

'There – you see?' said Mrs Winter. 'It helps them move really slowly and smoothly.'

Really, Mrs Winter was very clever!

One Saturday, two whole months after I'd started ballet classes, something strange happened.

At ten thirty all the pupils in my class piled into the community centre hall. But as well as Miss Cole and Mr Arthur there was a third person waiting for us. Up on the stage, someone had put a desk and a chair. And sitting on the chair was a tiny, frail-looking woman, dressed all in yellow. She was like a little wrinkled canary bird, and her thin pointed nose looked just like a beak.

I saw Belinda whisper to the girl beside her, as if she knew who the woman was. I thought Miss Cole would tell us before she began the class, but she didn't say anything, and acted as if the strange woman wasn't there.

It was difficult to concentrate on the exercises, while out of the corner of my eye, I was constantly catching a glimpse of yellow. From time to time, the woman scribbled on some paper in front of her, and when I saw her doing that, I was put off even more. It felt like a test. But what were we being tested on?

At the end of the class, I went up to Belinda.

'Who was that woman?' I whispered.

'That,' said Belinda importantly, 'was the scout from the Evanova School. She goes around the country watching classes. Then she invites people to audition for the school.'

The Evanova – hearing that name again sent a thrill through me. 'You said before Christmas that you were definitely going to audition. Has she picked you already?' I asked.

For the first time ever, I saw Belinda look uncomfortable. 'Not yet,' she admitted. Then she added defiantly, 'But she's bound to – you'll see.'

And she was right. The next Tuesday, Belinda came round to my house for tea. I hadn't wanted to invite her, but Mum had told me not to be silly.

'It's long overdue,' she'd said. 'Mrs Whitehead will think we're very rude.'

From the moment I saw Belinda standing on the doorstep, I knew what had happened. She had that smug look on her face. It didn't take her long to spill the beans.

'Mummy got a phone call last night from Miss Cole,' she said, reaching for another French Fancy cake – a pink one, of course. 'I've been chosen to audition for the Evanova, just like I said.'

'Well done!' said Mum, though I could see she thought Belinda was a bit boastful.

'Have many other people been chosen?' I asked. I ran through the class-list in my head. There really was no one quite as good as Belinda.

'Oh, I don't know.' Belinda pulled the icing off her cake, and pushed the sponge to the side of her plate. 'Mummy didn't ask. I should think I'm the only one.'

That night as I lay in bed, I tried to imagine what it must feel like to be Belinda; to be invited to audition for the Evanova! A proper ballet school . . . full-time training . . . and a real chance to become a ballerina. I couldn't help it: I was jealous. It was my dream – and it was coming true for someone else.

Seven

'Mum, Dad!' I thought I was going to burst. 'Guess what! Oh, quick, guess what, guess what!'

It was the next Saturday, and I'd had a lift home from ballet with Mrs Whitehead. I'd had to hold in my news all the way home, and the excitement had made me so wriggly that Belinda had asked sourly whether I had ants in my pants.

'What is it, Tiger?' Dad picked me up and held me above his head, just like he did with the twins. I kicked my legs and squealed. Then my bag slipped out of my hands, scattering ballet shoes, hair pins, hairbrush and spare tights all over the kitchen floor.

'Steady on,' said Mum, who had Thomas and Oliver on her lap, and was trying to stop them from pulling her ponytail. They thought it was great fun.

Dad plonked me down on a chair. 'Well?' he said. He pushed his glasses up his nose, and looked at me expectantly.

I took a gulp of air. I hardly knew where to start. Then the words began tumbling out.

'After the class, when we'd done our curtsies, Miss Cole said "Sadie Marsh, I would like a word", and I had to go and talk to her, and she said it ever so quietly so no one else could hear, and she said I had to ask you, and it was very serious, and perhaps you wanted to go and talk to her about it, and she gave me her phone number for you to ring . . .' I scrabbled in my pockets, looking for the scrap of paper she'd given me. 'Oh yes!' I suddenly remembered. 'She said she would have rung us before only she'd lost our phone number – so I told her it and she wrote it down.'

Dad looked puzzled. 'Hang on a minute, Tiger,' he said. '*What* did Miss Cole say to you? *What* do we need to talk to her about?'

I'd missed out the most important bit. 'The Evanova School!' I said, still hardly able to believe it myself. 'One other person has been invited to audition – and it's me!'

Mum and Dad had as much trouble believing it as I did.

'But you've only just started lessons,' Mum pointed out.

'You don't have to have done any training at all to audition,' I explained, repeating what Miss Cole had told me, 'though most people who try for the school have. Miss Cole says it means I've done extra well to get selected.'

'I'm sure that's true,' said Dad, looking proud.

'We could never afford these fees,' said Mum. She was looking at the brochure Miss Cole had given me. 'Not unless I got a job, anyway. And I can't work full-time until the twins are three at least.' She put a hand through her hair and looked worried. 'And it says it's a boarding school. You're too young for that, Sadie.'

'But I'm ten!' I protested.

'Exactly,' said Mum. 'Ten is too young to be away from home. And it's far too young to be devoting your life to one career. What if you get there and then change your mind about ballet?'

'I won't – I know I won't!' I said. 'Anyway, Mrs Winter says they do as much schoolwork at the Evanova as at a normal school. Dancers need to have a good education.'

'Mrs Winter?' said Dad. 'She seems to be behind everything these days.' I saw him and Mum exchange glances.

'We can't afford it, Sadie,' said Mum, looking at me seriously. 'Perhaps next year, eh?'

'But I'm the right age *now* to start in the first year!' I protested. 'It says they hardly ever take new pupils after that, at least not until they're sixteen.'

Dad was peering at the small print in the brochure. 'She's right,' he said to Mum. 'It does say that. Should we go and see Miss Cole, at least, and talk it over?'

Mum frowned at him. 'All right,' she said wearily. 'But I think you're raising false hopes, Simon. It isn't fair on Sadie when we're going to have to say no anyway.'

'One step at a time,' said Dad. Then he winked at me. 'Sounds like a good motto for a dancer, doesn't it?'

Eight

'Goal! Yeey!' shouted Tina, punching her fist in the air.

Tina's our babysitter and she's mad about football. If there's a game on when she's round, we have to watch it, no matter what. And this particular Sunday afternoon there was a match on Channel Four between two Italian teams. Tina kept waving her arms and shouting things at the TV, which made the twins giggle so much they both got hiccups.

I couldn't bear it. I was all jangled up inside, thinking about Mum and Dad being round at Miss Cole's for tea this very minute, talking about me and the Evanova School and whether I could audition for it. Just five minutes after they'd gone I'd started looking at the clock and wondering when they'd be back. The time was going so slowly, and the football didn't help. If there'd been a film on – a musical, perhaps, or one with a really exciting story that sweeps you along – I might not have fidgeted so much.

'What's up, Sado?' said Tina. 'Guinea pigs given you fleas?'

'Fleas, wees, hee hee hee.' Thomas and Oliver, only just recovered from the last bout of giggling, were off again.

I couldn't bear it. 'Don't be so stupid!' I shouted, and ran out of the room.

I sprinted all the way up to the attic and flung myself on my bed. I felt guilty for being rude, but I couldn't bear Tina's teasing, not today.

It seemed like years before I heard the front door go, and Mum's voice calling to Tina that they were back. I sat up, my heart pounding. Would they come up and tell me? What would they say?

But there were no footsteps on the stairs. I heard Tina's voice, and the front door went again. Then it was quiet. Slowly, I swung my legs off the bed and stood up. Then I made my way downstairs.

I found Dad in the kitchen. Mum was in the sitting-room, telling the twins that they were overtired and needed a nap. They didn't agree.

'Hello, Tiger,' said Dad, hanging his wet coat over the back of a chair near the boiler so it could dry. 'Your Miss Cole's very nice. She had those little chocolate slices you get from Mr Baxter's. I think I ate more of them than was polite.'

'You did!' called Mum from the other room.

'What did she say?' I asked.

'She thinks a lot of you, you know,' said Dad. 'Says you're a very quick learner, and you've got real promise. She thinks you should have the chance to audition.'

'But what about the money?' I hadn't forgotten Mum's worries.

'Well . . .' Dad sat down and started picking something off his jumper. 'Apparently there are a few scholarships available, though not many. You might be able to get one of those. But they'd have to think you were terribly good.'

'So I *can* audition?' I asked.

'We think you should have the chance, yes,' said Dad.

'But you mustn't build your hopes up, love.' Mum came in and put her arm round me. She gave me a squeeze. 'There must be hundreds and hundreds of children all over the country who want to go to that school. And Miss Cole told us that they only have places for about thirty each year, quite apart from this scholarship business. Just think how many that leaves disappointed . . .'

I didn't want to think – I couldn't bear to. All I knew was that three months ago I'd been dreaming about just starting ballet lessons – and now here I was, about to audition for the Evanova. That meant *anything* was possible.

Nine

Before ballet the next Saturday, I rushed up to Belinda – I wanted to impress her with my news. She couldn't think I was a baby beginner any longer.

'Guess what?' I said. 'I've been asked to audition for the Evanova too!'

I waited for the congratulations. But there was silence. 'You?' Belinda looked as if someone had wafted a bad egg under her nose. 'What a silly idea. You'll never get in, not in a million years.'

She tossed her blonde curls and walked off to the other side of the waiting room. 'Well, I can only try,' I said to myself stubbornly. I couldn't believe she wasn't even a little bit pleased for me.

After our class, Miss Cole said that Belinda and I should stay behind for a moment.

She waited till the other children had gone, then turned to us. 'Now,' she said, 'you have both done extremely well to be selected for this audition. But we have only five weeks to prepare for it. So, if your parents agree, I would like to give you some extra coaching. They will be free of charge – if one of you gets a place at the Evanova School, the honour will be reward enough. I hope you are both ready to work very hard?'

'Yes, Miss Cole,' we said in unison. Belinda gave me a frosty look.

'Will Thursday evenings at five thirty be convenient?' said Miss Cole. 'Please ask your parents to telephone me to confirm. I would like to start this week.'

'Yes, Miss Cole.' Belinda and I bobbed a little curtsey and ran to get our bags.

'Sadie, your hands look like wet lettuces!' said Miss Cole sharply.

I tried to hold them better: the fingers softly curled, but not limp; the wrists held steady, but not strained.

'And point those feet! Harder!'

There was so much to think about all at once! I saw Belinda look at me pityingly, as if she would never make such silly mistakes. But the next moment, Miss Cole called her to attention.

'Mind that banana back, Belinda! I've told you before!'

I loved the extra coaching, even though it was such hard work. It was wonderful to have Miss Cole's attention almost entirely to myself; it meant she told me off for more things, of course, but I didn't mind. I wanted to know what mistakes I was making, and although sometimes I was almost ready to cry when I couldn't get something just how Miss Cole wanted, it was because I was frustrated, not because I was upset.

I still went to my normal lessons on Saturdays, of

course. And I still did my practice at home. I practised my *développés* to build strength in my legs, and my *grands battements* to help keep me supple. I practised my *relevés* and tried to get better at not wobbling, and I practised my jumps and tried not to stick my bottom out when I landed, even when I was really tired and gasping for breath. And my favourite – *port de bras* – I practised that too, even while I was standing in the checkout queue at the supermarket with Dad. Mum would have cringed with embarrassment, but Dad didn't care – and neither did I. The slow, graceful movement of my arms made me feel dreamy, and I really could imagine being a Sleeping Beauty, then, or a Swan Princess – until Dad called me to help him put the shopping into bags.

'You've got a real little ballerina there,' said the lady on the till as Dad handed her the money.

'I know,' said Dad, and I beamed with pride.

One morning, a big brown envelope arrived, addressed to my parents.

'It's from the Evanova,' said Mum, looking at the crest on the back as she tore it open.

'What is it? What does it say?' I asked eagerly.

Mum pulled a handful of papers out of the envelope and looked through them.

'Forms to fill in – why they need three different ones I don't know . . .' she muttered. 'Oh, and this is about the audition.'

She was quiet for a moment and I watched her

eyes flick back and forth over the paper. She reads really fast.

'The audition's on the 17th and 18th. Hmmm . . .' Mum crossed the kitchen to where the calendar hung on the wall. 'Ah, fine,' she said. 'It's the first weekend of your Easter holidays.'

'A whole weekend?' I asked.

Mum nodded. 'And they want you to get there on the Friday evening. So you'll be staying at the school for two nights.'

'On my own?' I tried to make my voice sound unconcerned.

Mum looked at me. 'Yes. Is that all right?'

Quickly, I nodded. 'Great!'

Actually, the thought of it made me feel sick with nerves. But how could I tell Mum? She already thought boarding was a bad idea. If I told her I was scared about one weekend, how could I ever persuade her I would be all right away from home for a whole term at a time?

Mum tried to play the whole thing down. 'Just think of it as an adventure,' she kept saying. 'The audition itself is an experience not many people are lucky enough to have.'

I could tell she thought I wouldn't get in. She wouldn't even buy me any new ballet clothes. 'The brochure says you can wear whatever you have,' she pointed out. 'It's a waste to spend money on something you might only need once.'

'But Mum!' I pleaded. 'I heard Belinda telling

Sarah she's having a new leotard *and* new ballet shoes. I don't even have pink satins!'

Mum had a determined expression on her face. 'There are plenty of people whose parents don't buy them whatever they want. Belinda's more likely to be the odd one out, not you.'

So I had to settle for my old green leotard and my leather shoes with the elastic.

And to be honest, as the weeks went by, I began to think that Mum was right. I'd only been going to ballet since January; what chance did I stand of getting into a school like the Evanova? It was just a silly dream.

Ten

How Belinda's mum and my mum managed not to notice that the two of us didn't like each other, I don't know. But they obviously didn't.

'That was Audrey Whitehead,' said Mum, putting down the phone one evening the week before the audition. 'She's suggested that since you and Belinda are both going to the Evanova, you could go together. And she's offered to drive.'

'Oh Mum!' I wailed. 'I can't go with Belinda!'

'Why ever not?'

'She's horrid to me, that's why not.'

Mum looked stern. 'Now, don't be silly, Sadie. Just because you and Belinda have had a little tiff doesn't mean we should turn down Audrey's kind offer. You will have forgotten what it was all about by Friday night.'

'No, I–'

'Look,' Mum interrupted me. 'If Audrey doesn't take you, Dad will have to cancel a talk he's giving at the university. I can't go – I'll be at the old people's home. Please don't make a fuss.'

I shut up after that. There's not a lot you can say to Mum when she's decided you're going to do something.

* * *

Friday was the last day of the spring term, and our class was going on a trip to a place called Upthorpe Manor. I was glad – sitting in lessons all day, I would have got very nervous, but the trip was fun and it took my mind off things.

Robbie was in her element. Even though we didn't have to, she took a notebook with her and wrote down all the things we saw.

On the coach on the way back, Robbie and I had seats together, and we started talking about the audition for the first time that day. I'd never thought about it before, but I suddenly realised that if I got a place at the Evanova School, it would mean I would only see Robbie in the holidays. It was a horrible thought.

'We can write lots of letters,' said Robbie comfortingly, though she looked sad. 'If you're going to be a dancer, your training is the most important thing. If I had to go away to be a history professor, I'd do it too.'

And suddenly I remembered what Mrs Winter had said about having to sacrifice things for ballet. It looked like she was right.

We were due back at school for four o'clock, which would give me plenty of time to get home, check everything in my bag (which I'd packed the night before), and wait for Mrs Whitehead to pick me up at five. We were supposed to be at the Evanova School by half past six, though the audition wasn't going to be until the next day. I wondered whether

Belinda was feeling as nervous as me.

But then disaster struck halfway through the journey. Robbie and I were deep in a game of Scissors-paper-stone.

'Ouch! That was my hit! Scissors cut stone!'

'No they don't, silly! Stone blunts scissors.'

Suddenly Adam Perkins started waving his arms about.

'Miss, Miss! There's a load of black smoke coming out the bottom of the bus. Is it going to explode?'

'Bet there isn't, Miss,' said Samantha Jackson. 'Bet he's making it up.'

'Am not!'

'You are!'

'Adam! Samantha!' said Mrs Turner. 'Be quiet, both of you!'

Something was wrong, though, because the next minute the driver pulled over into a layby. Mrs Turner had a word with him and then she said, 'Simmer down, everyone. Just keep quiet while we sort out the problem.'

Only they didn't sort it out – they couldn't. The driver got the bonnet up, and spent ages bent under it. When he emerged, his hands were filthy, and he had black grease down his jacket, too. But still the bus wouldn't start. The driver had a word with Mrs Turner, and then he climbed out and walked off down the road.

'Where's he going, Miss?' asked Adam Perkins.

'He's going to phone the breakdown service,' said

Mrs Turner. 'Don't worry – they'll get here soon.' But Mrs Turner looked worried – very worried indeed.

'We broke down on the way to Spain once,' said Katie Platt. 'It was in a storm and we had to sleep in the car. Then we had Mars bars for breakfast 'cos that was all we'd got, and my little sister was sick *everywhere*—'

'All right, Katie, that will do,' said Mrs Turner.

Most of our class thought breaking down was great fun – and at first I did too. But then it struck me: it was just gone half past three now, and I didn't recognise the road we were on, so I knew there was some way to go before we got back to school. What if we didn't get back by four o'clock? I would have to run home, and I wouldn't have time to check my things. Then an even worse thought struck me: what if we didn't even get home by *five*? Would Mrs Whitehead wait for me? What if she went without me?

'Oh Robbie!' I said, clutching her arm suddenly. 'What am I going to do?'

Eleven

In the end it was nearly six o'clock before we got back to school, and I was trying very hard not to cry.

I'd told Mrs Turner that I absolutely had to be home by five, but she'd got quite cross with me.

'I'm aware you have an audition to go to, Sadie, but what do you expect me to do about it? We're all in the same boat, you know.'

When the bus driver got back from ringing the breakdown people, Mrs Turner went to ring the headmaster, so that he could tell the parents who turned up at school what had happened.

'Perhaps she could ring Mrs Whitehead too,' I said to Robbie.

'Go and ask her, then,' Robbie urged.

I stood up, but then sat down again.

Robbie frowned at me. 'What's the problem?'

'I don't have Mrs Whitehead's number,' I wailed.

'Never mind. She'll wait for you, I expect,' said Robbie, but as the minutes ticked by she looked less and less convinced.

The breakdown lorry took ages to arrive, and then they hitched the minibus to the back of it, and towed us slowly home. When we got to school, the headmaster was waiting outside, surrounded by a huddle of worried-looking parents. A little cheer went up as we rounded the corner. As soon as the bus came to a halt, I pushed along the aisle so I could be the first out.

'Sadie Marsh! Don't be so rude!' snapped Mrs Turner. 'What has got into you?' But by that time the door was open; I leapt down the steps and sprinted off along the road.

I reached home panting and leant hard on the doorbell. Tina opened the door.

'There you are!' she said, beaming. 'I wondered where you'd got to!'

'Have they gone? Are they here?' I blurted, pushing past her and running into the sitting-room, and then the kitchen. 'Mrs Whitehead and Belinda – did they wait for me?'

'Blonde lady, is it?' asked Tina. I nodded. 'She called a long time ago. She waited a while – I made her a cup of tea – but eventually she said she was very sorry but she had to go.'

'No!' I dropped my schoolbag and put my hands over my face.

'What is it, Sado?' Tina crouched down beside me. I began to sob.

'Take me . . . audition . . . can't . . . Dad's got . . . talk . . .' I was crying so hard I didn't make much sense. Tina cuddled me until I calmed down.

'Can *you* take me, Tina?' I said at last, prodding in my pocket for a hanky. I couldn't find one, so I wiped my nose on my cuff instead.

'Take you where?'

'The Evanova School – my audition.'

Tina shook her head sadly. 'I haven't got a car. And anyway – I've got to be here to mind the twins. Sorry, Sado, there's nothing I can do.'

It was too terrible. I pushed myself away from her and ran upstairs. When she knocked on my bedroom door a few minutes later I just shouted, 'Go away!' I didn't want to see anyone. I felt like the world had ended. All that hard work, all my dreams – ruined.

I don't think I've ever cried for so long. My eyes went puffy, and my nose got sore. Eventually, I found I couldn't cry any more, even though that was all I wanted to do – it was as if I had run out of tears.

The little clock on my bedside table ticked on, the hands passing seven o'clock, and then eight. I wondered what Belinda was doing – she would be at the school by now. That set me off crying again.

Then suddenly there was a tap at my door. I didn't have time to answer before it flew open. It was Dad, back from his talk.

'Tiger!' he said, rushing forward. 'What happened? Tina says you missed your lift.'

I told him, in a muddled way, about the bus breaking down, and Mrs Whitehead waiting for a bit, but then having to go.

Dad got out his hanky and wiped my cheeks. Then he thought for a moment. 'Right,' he said. 'Where's that school brochure?'

It was on my bedside table. I kept it there so that it

was the first thing I saw when I woke up every morning. I handed it to Dad.

He turned straight to the back. There was a map, and the school was marked with a red dot.

'Uh-huh,' said Dad, studying it. Then he checked his watch and stood up.

'Bag all packed?' he asked. I nodded. 'Good,' he said. 'Because we're going. Right now.'

I wanted to give Dad a great big hug for being a hero – but there wasn't time. He flew downstairs and asked Tina if she could stay until Mum got back. Tina said um and ah and looked at her watch, but Dad said please really desperately, and then she said yes.

Two seconds later, Dad and I were in the car, and he was starting up the engine.

It was dark and it was raining, and one of the windscreen wipers was on the blink. Dad leant forward over the steering-wheel, and peered at the road signs through the rain as we passed. I was praying that he knew the way, but I didn't want to ask in case I put him off and he missed something important.

'Don't worry,' said Dad every so often, 'we'll get you there.' But I soon worked out he said this every time he'd just taken a wrong turning.

Despite Dad's mistakes, we did get there – eventually. The rain had stopped and I was feeling very sleepy by the time the car swung off the road and on to a tree-lined driveway.

'Wake up, Tiger – this is it,' he said.

My first sight of the Evanova School was just a big shape in the darkness, dimly lit by one small lamp above the entrance archway. But even so I recognised it – I'd stared so many times at that picture in the brochure. I leant forward to look up through the windscreen. There was the tower, rising high above the archway, and though I couldn't see them, I knew that there were little windows dotted in the tower wall, right up to the top.

'It's gone ten o'clock,' said Dad, switching off the engine and examining his watch by the light of the lamp outside. 'I hope the door's still open.'

I climbed out of the car, clutching my small red case. Together we crunched over the gravel driveway towards the entrance.

The archway ahead of us had fancy iron gates. They were shut. Dad shook them – but they were chained and fastened with a big padlock. We walked to the wall at each side to look for a bell, but there wasn't one. Peering through the gates, we could see that the only bell was next to the big wooden door set into the inside wall of the archway – and there was no way we could reach it.

'Ah,' said Dad, scratching his chin.

'Dad, I've got to–' I began.

'I know, I know, Tiger,' he said, ruffling my hair. 'We'll find a way in.'

There was a chink of light showing through a ground floor window to the left. We squelched through a flowerbed – muddy after all the rain – to look in. The curtains were drawn, but there was a little gap in the middle, and through it we could see a man sitting in a chair. He had his back to us, and he was facing a TV which was on full blast.

'He must be a night watchman,' said Dad. He rapped on the window with his knuckles. 'Hey!' he shouted. 'Hey! Let us in!'

I knocked and shouted too, but the man didn't move. Then his bald head nodded softly onto his chest. He was fast asleep.

'Useless!' muttered Dad, and we squelched back onto the gravel path.

'Right, Tiger,' said Dad, 'we'll have to walk round the building and see if there are any other lights on. Someone's bound to be still awake.'

So we set off. It was tricky, picking our way through the darkness, not sure quite what we might be treading on, yet having to look up all the time instead of down, to see if we could see a light.

The school building was massive – there were three storeys of windows, thin pointed arched ones set into the red brick. And all of them were dark. After a while Dad took my case from me, though it wasn't very heavy.

We walked a long way. I kept thinking we were about to come back to the entrance again, but Dad said we hadn't gone round enough corners.

'This is the back of the building,' he said. 'It's certainly a big place.'

Then – 'Look!' I cried, pointing up to a window on the first floor, a little way ahead of us. There was a dim light creeping out from behind the heavy curtains.

'Well spotted!' said Dad, and he bent down and started scratching around in the grass.

'Have you dropped something?' I said anxiously. It would have been just like Dad to lose his glasses or car keys at a moment like this.

'No, I'm – ah! This'll do – looking for a stone,' said Dad.

He took aim, and tossed it up against the window.

'Bit of an art, this,' he said, as he waited a moment, then bent to find another. 'You've got to throw it hard enough so it gets there, but not so hard it's in danger of breaking the glass.'

The stones made little 'pock' sounds as they bounced off the window. I was beginning to think that the person inside must be deaf, or asleep with the TV on like the night watchman, when suddenly the curtains were drawn back and, with a bit of difficulty, someone pulled the bottom half of the window up.

'Hey! What's going on?' came a loud whisper. It was a girl's voice, and I could see the outline of a small curly head against the light.

'Sorry to disturb you,' said Dad politely, in a loud whisper too. 'I'm here with my daughter, Sadie. We've arrived late for the audition and we can't get in.'

'Jeepers!' said the girl. Her accent had a strange twang to it. 'You're in a fix then!'

'Can you come down and let us in?' asked Dad.

'Not likely,' said the girl. 'Matron's been on the prowl, all the lights are out and I'd get lost in two seconds.'

'Oh.' Dad sounded a bit stumped.

'Tell you what, though,' said the girl. 'You could climb up here.'

Although it was only the first floor, it was quite a long way up. I waited for Dad to laugh and dismiss the idea.

But he didn't. He walked over to the wall, and seemed to be studying the drainpipe that ran up past the girl's window. I felt my stomach go tight.

'Dad–' I started.

'It's possible, Tiger,' he said, measuring himself against the wall. 'We've only got to get *you* up, after all. You could stand on my shoulders, then put your foot on that bracket there–' he pointed to a piece of metal pinning the drainpipe to the wall. 'Then you'd be able to get your arms over the windowsill, and the girl could pull you in.'

'The name's Luci,' whispered the girl, who'd been listening. 'With an "i".'

'Hello, Luci,' said Dad.

'I can't!' I protested.

'I'll be right underneath if anything goes wrong,' said Dad.

Mum always said Dad could be really silly

sometimes – now I was starting to agree.

Dad seemed to have guessed what I was thinking. 'Just don't tell your mother when you get home,' he whispered.

I looked at him, then up to the shadowy view of the girl's face above. They were both looking at me expectantly.

'Seems like you haven't got a choice,' said the girl, but in a friendly voice.

She was right. It was dark and cold, and the rest of the school had gone to bed. There would be no other way in until the morning.

'OK,' I said reluctantly.

'That's my brave Tiger,' said Dad, putting my case down, and stretching his hands out to me.

I gripped his arms, and he swung me high above his head. It took me a minute to get my feet firmly planted on his shoulders. 'Ouch!' said Dad in the darkness, and I realised that, with my outdoor shoes on, it probably hurt him quite a bit. He'd be covered in mud, too.

I straightened my legs, carefully, with quite a few wobbles, and steadied myself against the wall. Dad's fingers were digging into my legs.

'Now find the bracket for your foot,' he said, edging nearer to the drainpipe.

The pipe was clammy and cold, and there was a creeper growing up it that I was afraid I might get tangled in.

'Don't look down,' said Luci. I glanced up instead,

and saw her smiling at me reassuringly from surprisingly nearby.

I gripped the pipe in both hands and, feeling with one foot, I found the bracket. I tested it with my weight first, then wedged my foot in between the pipe and the wall, and pushed myself up so my leg was straight.

'Well done!' whispered Dad.

Luci was very near now. 'Get a hand over here,' she said, making space on the windowsill.

Taking a hand off the drainpipe was the last thing in the world I wanted to do, but I couldn't hang in mid-air all night, so I took a deep breath, gripped hard with my right hand, and moved my left over the windowsill. I could reach further than I thought, and my arm hooked right over, up to the elbow. Luci took a firm hold of it.

'I've got you,' she said. 'Now the other hand.'

This was the really scary bit. I was going to have to let go, and shift my weight sideways, away from the pipe, which would throw me off-balance. If I lost my grip on the windowsill . . .

'Come on,' Luci urged. 'Quick!'

I let go. Luci tightened her hold on my left arm and pulled me upwards with all her might. It was painful, but she held me well, and my right hand hooked over the sill with no trouble. I was almost half in the room now, with my head and shoulders hanging down towards the floor, and the hard edge of the window pressing into my stomach.

'Let your legs swing free, Tiger!' called Dad from below.

For one horrible moment I thought I couldn't. I'd wedged my foot so well between the drainpipe and the wall, that at first when I tugged it wouldn't come out.

'Oh! Oh! I'm stuck!' I panted, wiggling my leg this way and that. Then at last it came free, and with one last yank from Luci, I was bundled into the room, head first.

'You all right?' Her face, upside-down, peered at me as I lay in a heap on the carpet.

'Think so,' I said. My knees were sore – they'd got grazed on the wall – but that was all.

'She's OK!' whispered Luci to Dad through the window.

'Now for the bag!' he called back.

'Jeepers!' said Luci. I scrambled to my feet and peered out of the window beside her. Dad was holding up my little case.

'I can't climb up,' he said. 'The pipe won't be strong enough to hold my weight.' He bounced the case in his hands. 'And it's a bit heavy to throw.'

'Hang on!' Luci darted away from the window, and stood back, looking at the curtains.

'What?' I said anxiously. 'What is it?'

'Yep, it'll do,' said Luci to herself, and delved into a bag in the corner. She brought out a small pair of nail scissors. Then she drew a chair up beside the window, stood on it, and started working away with the scissors at the curtain cords that were dangling at the side of the window.

'You can't do that!' I said, horrified.

'Course I can,' said Luci. 'Mangy old curtains anyway.'

At last, she'd cut through them. She got down from the chair and leant out of the window again. Hanging on to one end of the cord, she dropped the other down to Dad.

'Right you are!' called Dad, understanding exactly what she meant him to do. He tied the end of the cord to the handle of my little case. Then he gave the thumbs-up, and Luci began to pull it in.

'Steady!' called Dad, as the case started swinging dangerously close to the ground floor window.

'What's in this thing?' muttered Luci, straining on the rope.

The little case had cleared the window below, and was just reaching the lip of our windowsill, when it caught on a bit of creeper.

'Blast!' said Luci, tugging at it harder. She tugged again, and staggered backwards as it came free and bounced up into view.

'Oh no!' I cried. With all the tugging, the fastening had come undone. As the lid of the case swung open, I dived towards it.

I just caught the edge of it, and narrowly avoided everything falling out and cascading down into the flowerbeds. But as I pulled the case into the room, I saw the edge of something slip away through the crack. Something green.

'My leotard!' I shrieked.

I peered down to where Dad stood in the shadows. 'Have you caught my leotard?' To my annoyance, Dad was laughing.

''Fraid not, Tiger. It's got caught . . .'

And then I saw it, dangling from the creeper a few metres below me – too low to reach, but too high for Dad to grab it.

'We'll need a long stick to hook that in,' said Luci, beside me. 'Don't worry,' she added, seeing my stricken expression, 'we'll do it in the morning. You can sleep in here with me tonight – I've got a spare bed – look.'

I scanned the room for the first time. It was small, with just enough space for a chest of drawers, a desk, and two single beds. One of them had the covers thrown back – the other was untouched.

Dad had caught the end of Luci's words. 'OK then,' he whispered up. 'I'd better get going.' I looked out at him. I'd forgotten that he had to drive all the way home again. 'Good luck, Tiger,' he said. 'Show 'em what you can do. I'll ring Mrs Whitehead to make sure she'll bring you back with Belinda on Sunday. And Luci – thanks for your help.'

Luci waved down to him. 'No sweat,' she said.

Twelve

'It's a good job I couldn't sleep,' said Luci as she shut the window and drew the curtains again. 'I'd only just put the light on, to see if reading would help.' She turned to me. 'Hey – you look shaken up. Take your coat off and sit down on the bed. How come you're so late, anyway?'

I told her the whole story. At the end she said, 'Jeepers! Your dad's brilliant, bringing you here like this. Mine would've just said "Tough luck – you missed it", I reckon.'

I thought that Mum would have said the same. But I knew that Dad bringing me wasn't my only piece of luck tonight. We would have been stuck outside in the cold if it hadn't been for Luci.

'You're Australian, aren't you?' I asked, a bit shyly. At last I'd worked out what the twang in her voice was.

'Ten out of ten!' she said. 'D'you think this school will be too English for me? It looks really old-fashioned.'

'You're auditioning too? I thought–' She seemed so confident, so at home. 'I thought you were a pupil here.'

'No,' she said. 'I just got here tonight.'

'Did you come all the way–'

'From Australia for this weekend?' she finished

for me, then laughed. 'No way! No – my folks live in London now. Well, my mum and sister and step-dad do. My real dad still lives in Sydney. We just came over this spring. No –' She yawned and clambered back under the bedclothes. '– if I was still back home I wouldn't be auditioning for this place, I'd be auditioning for the Sydney Ballet School. That's where I've always wanted to go.'

'Is it as good as here?' I asked. I could hardly believe that anyone might prefer to go somewhere else, no matter where they lived.

'I'll say!' said Luci robustly. 'Better, if you ask me, but I reckon I'm probably biased. I rate it as the best school in the whole of Australia, and Australia's heaps bigger than Great Britain, you know.'

I didn't see how that made any difference, but I said nothing.

'Mind you, I'd be happy enough to come here – if they'd have me,' went on Luci. 'Though I don't think I stand much chance.'

'Why not?'

'Well, my dancing's not bad,' she said candidly. 'But I just don't look right. You know there are some girls who look like classical dancers before they even do a step?'

I nodded, thinking wistfully.

'Well, I'm never going to be one of them. And the Evanova may be a brilliant school, but I've heard it's very traditional. Somehow I don't reckon they'll go for the likes of Luci Simpson.'

I could see what she meant. About my age – though a few centimetres taller – she had a round moon face, shiny-bright and dotted with freckles, like hundreds and thousands on a cake. Her hair was a rich orangey-brown, and was cut level with her chin. The most amazing thing about it was the way it curled – spiralling and corkscrewing in every direction at once.

But it wasn't just the curly short hair and freckles that were a million miles away from the usual idea of the sleek-headed ballerina. Even in her pyjamas, you could tell Luci was a more solid build than most dancers – she looked sporty rather than graceful. But if there was one thing I knew for certain, it was that I liked her.

Though I fell asleep almost the moment Luci turned the light out, I had a disturbed night. I kept half-waking, thinking I could hear rain outside and worrying about my leotard, flapping around on the creeper. When I did sleep, I dreamt – dreamt I was dangling from a cliff, with Luci hanging on to one of my hands and Dad hanging on to the other. Hard as they pulled, they just couldn't seem to drag me to the top . . .

I woke feeling exhausted.

'Hello, sleepyhead!' Luci was already up, in jeans and a hooded sweatshirt. She was tying the laces on her trainers.

'What's the time?' I asked, rubbing my eyes.

'Nearly seven,' she said brightly. 'The alarm bell

will go in a minute. We're supposed to be down at breakfast by half past.'

'What will I do?' I raised my head and leant on my elbows. 'No one knows I'm here yet.'

'That's true.' Luci came to sit beside me and frowned in thought. 'I don't think Miss Stretton would like the idea of you having climbed in, either.'

'Who's Miss Stretton?'

'The deputy headmistress,' said Luci, wrinkling her nose in disapproval. 'We had a welcoming talk from her last night. More of a telling off, actually, even though we'd only just got here.' She clasped her hands in front of her, and put on a thin, pinched English voice. ' "We insist on discipline and politeness at all times. Even if you are only here for one weekend, you will observe our rules." '

I giggled. 'She sounds horrible.'

'She hates me already,' said Luci ruefully. 'I made the mistake of whispering to someone while she was talking. I did it ever so quietly – but she must have supersonic hearing. "Child, do you have something to say?" she said, fixing me with this awful look.' Luci patted my bedspread. 'Anyway, you'd better watch out – she's just the type to try and expel someone before they've even got a place here!'

'What'll I do?' I already knew I could rely on Luci to think of something.

It only took a minute. 'I know!' she said. 'Get dressed and put your coat on – and pack everything in your case. Then sneak downstairs and present yourself in the entrance hall. Say you've just arrived – your parents couldn't bring you last night, and they had to drop you off this early because they're on their way somewhere. And if anyone notices you haven't come in through the front door, you can say you found your way in at the back by mistake.'

'Brilliant!' I jumped out of bed and grabbed my clothes. 'You're really quick with ideas.'

'Years of trying to avoid a telling off from my mum,' explained Luci with a grin. 'Teaches you to use your imagination.'

Thirteen

I got dressed swiftly and, with careful instructions from Luci about how to find my way downstairs, I was soon out in the corridor, clutching my little red case and pulling my duffle coat around me.

I was glad Luci had told me where to go – the corridors were like a maze. I could easily have ended up wandering around for hours and getting nowhere. As it was, I looked like someone out of an old spy movie – putting my back to the wall and peering round every corner before I made my next move, afraid that I might meet the dreaded Miss Stretton before I reached the ground floor.

I was lucky. Once the wake-up bell had sounded, a few sleepy figures started drifting towards the washrooms at the end of each corridor, but they hardly even had their eyes open, and none of them spotted me lurking in the shadows.

I found the wide spiral staircase with the grand red carpet that Luci had described, and hurried down it. I wondered for an instant how many times Lily Dempsey had run up and down the very same stairs when she'd been a pupil here.

Then I reached the ground floor. Cleanly swept corridors stretched away on all sides – but I knew the entrance hall lay straight ahead, so I didn't hesitate. As I hurried along I passed large double doors on either side of me, marked 'Library' and 'Old Hall'.

'Oof! Watch where you're going, *do*!'

I'd been so busy reading the labels on the doors that I hadn't noticed a figure rushing along the corridor in the opposite direction. By the time I turned my head, all I met was a purple and green woolly jumper, very close up.

'Sorry!' I said, as the person stepped back from me, patting her hair anxiously.

'Dear *me*, in such a hurry! Are you on your way out?' the woman asked, eyeing my coat and case. Then she bent and peered at me more closely. 'Now – I *didn't* see you yesterday, did I? I'm *very* good with faces, and yours I *don't* recognise.' Her head moved back and forth as she talked, like a nervous chicken.

'No,' I said, and hesitated as I ran through Luci's story again in my head. 'Um – I'm on my way in, not out. You see, I should have got here last night, but Mum and Dad couldn't bring me. They've just dropped me off now, and I found a door round the back–' I gestured vaguely behind me.

'Well!' The woman had a bundle of papers with her. She licked a finger and began to leaf through them. 'This is *most* irregular – we did request that all candidates should arrive by six thirty yesterday evening at the very *latest*–' Suddenly she stopped. 'You *are* for the audition, I suppose?'

I nodded enthusiastically.

'*Most* irregular,' said the woman again, making a small tutting noise. She found the right list and began to look along it. 'Name?'

'Sadie Marsh.'

'Ah . . . *Yes*.' Producing a pencil suddenly from behind her ear, the woman marked a neat tick on the list, then consulted a small clock that was hanging on a chain round her neck. 'You *are* in time for breakfast, Sadie Marsh. Do you require breakfast?'

'Yes, please. We had to leave so early I–'

'I will take you to your room, then you can proceed to the dining hall with the other candidates. *I*, by the way –' she drew herself up a little taller, '– am Miss Featherstone, the school secretary.'

'Nice to meet you,' I said politely, holding out my hand.

For some reason, this seemed to startle Miss Featherstone. She didn't take my hand, but made a small alarmed gobbling noise instead, turned on her heel, and hurried off down the corridor. Not quite certain of what to do, I followed her.

Breathing rapidly, Miss Featherstone led me up the same spiral staircase I'd just descended, and back into the maze of first floor corridors. The sleepy figures I'd seen a few moments before were nearly all dressed now, darting in and out of their rooms with hairbrushes and sponge bags. Some were already making their way down to the dining hall for breakfast.

When Miss Featherstone finally came to a halt, I could hardly believe it: she had stopped at Luci's room.

'C23,' she said to herself, and made another little tick on her list. She rapped sharply on the door, and then opened it.

'Good morning, Miss Featherstone,' I heard Luci say.

'Luci Simpson, your roommate *has* arrived after all,' said Miss Featherstone. 'Regrettably *late* – what Miss Stretton will say about it I *don't* know. I wonder if you would escort her to the dining hall for breakfast?'

'Of course, Miss Featherstone,' said Luci's voice.

'Sadie Marsh, you may come in.' Miss Featherstone beckoned to me.

'Hello, Sadie Marsh,' said Luci, shaking my hand, and somehow managing to keep a straight face. 'Very nice to meet you.'

Fourteen

'I talked to two girls at supper last night – I must introduce you to them.'

Luci was leading me along the corridor on our way to the dining hall for breakfast. I wanted to stop and look at the pictures on the walls – they were all of dancers – but Luci was walking so briskly I didn't have a chance.

'Their names are Ella and Pippa,' Luci went on. 'Ella's great, but Pippa's terribly stuck-up. She's the daughter of Clara Parnell, though, so I guess she's got a right to be.'

'*The* Clara Parnell?' I asked, amazed. I'd read about her in my library books. She'd been a ballerina, famous all over the world, until a bad injury a few years ago had put an end to her career.

'Yes, *the* one,' said Luci. 'You can see the resemblance, too. Pippa's got the same long legs and those really elegant hands. What I wouldn't give to look like that!'

'Me too!'

The dining hall was vast, with a really high ceiling and large arched windows. It made me think of a church. There were lots of big tables set out in rows, with long wooden benches down each side of them.

'Are all these people here for the audition?' I asked.

Three of the tables were full already, though some of the people having breakfast looked a lot older than me.

'Most of them,' said Luci, taking a bowl and spoon and putting them on her tray. 'But the older ones are the school's fourth and fifth formers. They've got big exams next term, so they're here for extra coaching.'

I was amazed Luci knew so much, even though she'd only arrived last night.

'There they are!' Luci was waving to someone on the furthest table. 'Come on.' She set off with her tray, and I followed her.

'I'm Gabriella Bruni – but most people call me Ella,' said the first girl, holding out her hand politely. I shook it; it felt tiny, but her handshake was firm. 'And this is Pippa Parnell-James.' The girl next to her looked up, and nodded to me, her lips curved in a half-smile.

'Sadie got here a bit late last night,' explained Luci.

'You didn't miss anything,' said Pippa. Then she spotted my plate. 'Brave girl,' she remarked drily. 'Not many *dancers* put away breakfasts like that.'

I admit, I did have quite a lot: sausages, bacon, bread and butter, and baked beans. I never ate cooked breakfasts at home but, having missed supper last night, I was ravenous. I looked at Pippa's plate. She had a tiny helping of muesli, and one piece of toast without butter or jam.

Luci dug me in the ribs when Pippa wasn't looking

and made a take-no-notice face. But I must admit, I rather went off the food after that.

The conversation soon turned to the auditions. They were to be held in the afternoon – the morning would be taken up with individual medical examinations.

'I didn't know we were having medicals,' I said.

'Oh yes,' said Luci. Then she put on a pretend solemn voice: 'They have to check if we're sound physical specimens, suitable for the stresses and strains of ballet training. And if we're going to grow into the right shape and height too.'

'Really?' I'd had no idea about this. 'You mean, we might fail the medical, and not get a place here however well we dance?'

'It's possible, I guess,' admitted Luci. 'Though if you're going to grow too tall or too short they might take you on anyway if you're really really good. Think of Wayne Sleep.'

'Wayne–?'

Luci looked surprised I hadn't heard of him. 'He used to dance with the Royal Ballet. He was much shorter than most male dancers, but he was brilliant.'

'It's this afternoon I'm really worried about,' said Ella. 'I haven't slept properly all week.'

Ella was exactly what Luci had been talking about last night – one of those people who looks perfect for ballet. She was small – not just in height, but in everything; her hands, wrists, feet . . . even her nose and ears looked delicate. She had jet black hair, tied in a ponytail at the back, which tapered like the end of an artist's paintbrush. Her eyes were dark too, and had really long lashes, which made them seem enormous in her fragile, heartshaped face. Beside her, I felt gawky and plain.

Pippa was quite different, but looked every inch the dancer too. She was bigger than Ella, but very slim. Her face was long, with a small pointed chin and a straight, bony nose. Luci was right – you could see she looked like her mother.

And Pippa was the only one amongst us who didn't seem nervous about the audition at all.

'Why should I be?' she said, sounding surprised at the idea when I asked her. 'They won't set us anything difficult – I could do it with my eyes shut. After all, there are probably some people here who haven't done much ballet before. The school has to look at them now they've come all this way, though it must be a terrible waste of time . . .'

I tried desperately not to blush. She seemed to be talking about me. How did she know? Could she tell just by looking at me how inexperienced I was? I wondered if it would be obvious at the audition, too. 'Sadie Marsh,' they'd say, 'why are you wasting our time? You hardly know anything . . .'

Just then my thoughts were interrupted by the sight of Belinda, sitting at another table. She didn't seem to have anyone to talk to and, on the spur of the moment, I waved.

I know she saw me, because she looked shocked

for a moment that I was there. But then she pretended she was looking at something else, and turned her head away.

'Someone you know?' asked Luci, following my gaze.

I felt a bit hurt, but I didn't want to show it. 'Oh, just a girl from the same ballet class as me,' I shrugged. 'We're not great friends.'

After breakfast, Luci, Ella, Pippa and I left the dining hall together. Luci showed me the noticeboard where all the lists for the medicals, auditions, and the next day's interviews were pinned up.

'See,' said Luci, pointing to my name. 'Your medical's at nine forty-five. I'm not until eleven. And we're in different groups for the audition, too.'

The auditions were happening at half past two, and the candidates had been divided into groups.

'I wish we were together,' I said to Luci. 'Though I'm glad I'm with you, Ella.' Ella smiled.

'Yes,' said Luci pointedly, 'I'm beginning to feel this isn't my lucky weekend.' She was in the same group as Pippa.

'I don't care who's in my group,' Pippa announced. 'When I'm dancing I'm not aware of anyone else at all.'

'That'd make a *pas de deux* pretty tricky,' muttered Luci under her breath.

With all this talk of the audition, a terrible thought struck me. 'My leotard!' I said suddenly. 'It's still on the creeper!'

Ella and Pippa looked puzzled, so I hurriedly explained what had happened the night before. Ella's eyes widened in amazement. 'You climbed in?'

'Shh!' said Luci. 'You never know who's listening. Come on.'

A minute later we were upstairs and making our way along C corridor. 'We need a stick,' said Luci. 'Hey! This'll do!'

She'd found a wooden pole standing against the wall, with a brass hook at one end.

'What is it?' asked Ella.

'It's for opening these windows at the top, see?' Luci held it up, and demonstrated how the hook fitted into catches on the small windows above each casement.

'It's perfect!' I said. 'Luci – you're a genius!'

'You'll get into frightful trouble if anyone sees you with it,' said Pippa, sounding vaguely bored. I could tell she didn't think getting my leotard back was very important. I wondered why she was bothering to tag along at all.

'I'm going to bring it back, though, aren't I?' Luci glanced at Pippa impatiently. Then she raced off along the corridor, with the rest of us in pursuit.

We reached the door of C23, went in, and flung the window open. For a moment as I looked out I was afraid the leotard had blown away – but then I saw it, flapping gently as the wind gusted around it.

'Now – someone hang on to my waist,' said Luci. I

obliged, and then Ella grabbed my waist, just in case. Pippa sat on the bed.

The pole was heavy and unwieldy, and Luci had difficulty aiming it. She puffed away, saying, 'Nearly!' and 'Oh, blast it!' several times, before at last she said, 'That's it!' and began to pull the pole back in.

'Thanks ever so much,' I said gratefully, as the scrap of green appeared back through the window. Then, as I examined the leotard more closely, my face fell. 'Oh no!'

It was in a dreadful state: smeared with dirt in several places, and with a big rip down one side.

'It must have got caught,' said Luci apologetically. 'I did have to tug a bit.'

I sat down heavily on my bed. 'I don't have another. What shall I wear for the audition?'

'I've got a spare,' said Luci, 'but it's a bit big even for me . . . Hang on.' She rummaged in her bag, and pulled out a bright red leotard.

'Mmm, that's nice,' said Pippa in a sarcastic tone.

Luci ignored her and held it up against me. 'Enormous,' she said miserably. 'It'll look dreadful.'

'I've only got one, I'm afraid,' said Ella.

'Well,' Luci folded up the red leotard. 'That just leaves . . .'

All eyes turned to Pippa. 'Me?' she said, incredulous. 'You want *me* to let Sadie wear one of mine?'

'I'd be ever so grateful,' I said humbly.

Pippa sighed. 'Oh, very well.' She pushed herself

off the bed and stood up. 'Come on. Let's sort it out before the medicals start.'

I grinned. Secretly I felt rather honoured at the idea of borrowing something from the daughter of Clara Parnell.

We made our way to Pippa and Ella's room on the floor above, putting the pole back where Luci had found it on the way.

'Terribly poky, these rooms,' remarked Pippa as we went in. 'When I'm a pupil here I shall expect a room to myself.'

I noticed Ella looked a little hurt at that. Luci mouthed '*When*?' silently behind Pippa's back and raised her eyebrows.

It turned out Pippa had brought four leotards with her. 'I couldn't decide,' she said defensively, seeing the look on Luci's face.

She didn't let me choose, though. 'Here, have this one,' she said, holding out a pale turquoise leotard made of shiny lycra, with delicate little shoulder straps.

'It's lovely,' I said, looking at it in wonder.

'Well, wash it tonight before you give it back,' said Pippa. Then, as if suddenly worried that she'd sounded a little sharp, she smiled tightly. 'Please.'

Fifteen

At a quarter to ten I knocked on the door marked 'Doctor's Office'.

'Come in,' said a muffled voice. I turned the handle.

The room was light and airy, with a high padded bench to the left, a folding screen to the right and, in the centre, a desk. Behind it sat a large woman in a white coat, with a stethoscope round her neck. She got up when she saw me.

'I'm Doctor Payne,' she said, and the stethoscope bounced up and down as she gave a throaty chuckle. 'Horrid name for a doctor, isn't it?'

I liked Doctor Payne. She looked more like a farmer to me than a doctor, with her big strong hands and plump rosy cheeks. I could just imagine her in a pair of wellies stomping through a muddy field – and the thought distracted me so much that I even forgot to be embarrassed when I had to take off my top and skirt and stand there in my knickers.

I had to touch my toes while the doctor looked very carefully at my spine. Then I lay on the padded bench as she lifted my legs one by one and spent a long time studying my feet.

When she saw my grazed knees and scratched shins, Doctor Payne made a whistling sound through her teeth. 'Took a tumble did you?'

I nodded. 'In the playground at school.'

The doctor wiped the scratches with cotton-wool soaked in something stingy. 'Nothing serious,' she said. 'But a dancer should learn to look after herself better.' She tapped my legs. 'These – they'll be your livelihood one day.' And she smiled.

'I don't care how nice Doctor Payne was, I hate being prodded and poked!' said Luci when we were all together again in the dining hall at lunch-time. She was taking revenge by poking the piece of boiled fish on her plate.

'Doctor Payne exclaimed over my feet,' said Pippa proudly. 'But then I do have remarkable arches.'

'Let's see!' I said. I leant round the side of the table as Pippa slipped off one of her shoes and pointed her foot. It was true – it did make the most beautiful curved shape. I could just see it in a proper pointe shoe, supporting Pippa as she balanced in a graceful *arabesque*.

'Pwoh!' Luci held her nose and pretended to swoon.

'My feet do not smell,' said Pippa hotly, stuffing her foot back into her shoe.

'Where do we change into our practice clothes for the audition?' asked Ella.

'In our rooms, I guess,' said Luci. 'Sadie, will you help me with my hair? Squashing it into a hairnet is like trying to persuade two hundred wriggling eels into a string bag.'

'As long as you'll help me with mine,' I said.

Luci smiled. 'It's a deal.'

After lunch the four of us split up to go to our different rooms. Luci was right: it was a struggle to get her crazy curls to go just where you wanted, but once they were tucked inside the thick brown hairnet, and the hairband was in place holding her fringe back, the overall effect was surprisingly neat.

She had a bit of trouble with my hair, too. It was obvious she'd never done a bun before, and there was quite a bit of 'Hang on!' and 'Whoops!' and 'Oh blast, another bit's escaped!' – but at last it was finished. And though when I put my hand up and felt it, it *did* seem a little lumpy, and I could have sworn it wasn't *quite* in the centre of my head, still it seemed solid enough – and it was an awful lot better than anything I could have managed by myself!

At last it was time to go downstairs. I was bound for Dempsey Studio and Luci for Tyrrel Studio – so we said goodbye to each other at the bottom of the stairs.

'Go get 'em!' said Luci with a wink. I smiled back as confidently as I could.

To tell you the truth, I was petrified. Nerves make me shivery, and as I pushed against the heavy studio door, I wished I'd brought my cardigan with me to wear until the audition started. But I didn't dare go all the way back to my room, in case it made me late.

The studio must have been about three times as big as the community centre hall Miss Cole taught in. A double barre ran along three walls; the top barre was meant for taller people and the bottom barre for smaller ones. Above them hung framed pictures, showing dancers taking curtain calls on vast stages, or posing in perfect arabesques and attitudes in front of painted theatre backdrops.

At any other time I would have loved to spend ages examining each one. But I was too nervous to concentrate on anything just now. I'd brought my character shoes with me – red shoes with a small heel and a button fastening – in case we needed them, and I put them down in the corner behind the grand piano. Then I went to the back of the room and stood at the barre. I tried to concentrate on doing some *pliés* in first position to warm up, remembering all the things Miss Cole had taught me: straight back, bottom in, knees over toes, don't look down.

The studio door swung open, shut and open again as more and more candidates came into the room. I snatched glances at them: the boys in their white T-shirts, black leggings and soft black shoes, and the girls in their pink tights and leotards of all colours – blue, green, black, red and purple.

'Room for me?' said a voice suddenly at my elbow.

I was grateful to see Ella's friendly smile and gladly made space for her. She looked perfect in her black leotard and her shiny hair was pulled back into an expert bun. With a final touch of style, she had pinned two tiny white flowers to the top of it. I wished I'd thought of something like that – and I suddenly realised I should have practised doing my hair at home. What chance would I stand alongside someone like Ella, who already looked like a real dancer?

But my worrying was interrupted a moment later as all eyes turned to the front of the room: Miss Featherstone had come in. She was clutching a clipboard, a small box and a pile of little squares of white material.

'Group One,' she addressed us in a strained, quavering voice. 'Here are your candidate *numbers*.' She held up the little squares. 'You must pin one to the *front* and one to the *back* of your leotards or T-shirts. Help each other – I haven't time to pin you all.'

She set down the squares and the little box – which turned out to be full of safety pins – on a table beside the piano.

'I will read out *each* name in *turn*,' she said, pulling her pencil from behind her ear and holding it ready above the clipboard. 'At the sound of your name, please come *forward* to collect your numbers. Jennifer *Adams* . . .'

I was number eighteen; Ella was five. We helped each other with the pins, and I noticed that Ella's fingers were trembling. She must have been as nervous as I was.

When we were finished I looked to the front of the room again. Miss Featherstone had been replaced by a young woman with sandy hair and those strange T-bar shoes that Miss Cole wears.

'I'm Miss Partridge,' she said with a friendly smile. 'I'll be taking your audition. This is Mrs Bates –' she gestured to a woman who was just settling herself at the piano '– and these are Miss Levange and Mrs Seymour.' Two other ladies had come in and sat down at the table. I recognised one: Miss Levange was the bird-like woman who had come to Miss Cole's and had chosen Belinda and me for this audition. She wasn't wearing bright yellow though – today she was dressed from head to toe in brilliant green.

And so the audition began. To my surprise, it didn't start off at the barre like a normal class, with *pliés* and *battements tendus* and all the other familiar exercises. Instead, Miss Partridge asked us to come straight into the centre and find a space. She gave us a funny exercise to do: knee bends with our feet facing forwards, rather than to the side like in normal first position.

Then we had to sit on the floor and do several other exercises. We pointed and turned up our toes, circled our ankles and, lying flat, we kicked our legs as high as we could. We had to show our best 'frogs' legs', too. That's when you lie on your back, bend your knees up and let them drop open, to see if you can get them on to the floor without straining or arching your back. It tests how much you can turn your legs to face sideways right from the hip socket – it's called your natural 'turn-out'. It's very important for ballet. Some people in the class found it difficult, but luckily I knew this was one thing I could do.

Then, at last, we started to do some proper ballet steps. Miss Partridge made up a lovely *enchaînement* – partly *port de bras* and partly slow *adagio* movements – and Mrs Bates played a beautiful tune to go with it. I really enjoyed that. I forgot about the audition and the strange examiners and just got lost in the music, like I did at Miss Cole's.

But it didn't last for long. 'Now let's swap over; everyone in the back half of the room come to the front,' Miss Partridge said. The whole of the back row froze in horror. We were at the back because we *wanted* to be; we were the nervous ones, and we'd been quite happy to let the confident dancers – and the ones who simply liked showing off – fill up the front. The last thing we wanted to do now was swap places with them.

We edged reluctantly forwards. Miss Partridge laughed. 'Come on now, I won't bite,' she said. She grabbed several people and pulled them towards her. She put me right in the middle of the front row, practically under Miss Levange's nose. I thought I was going to faint with nerves.

When the music for the exercise began again, I couldn't concentrate properly. Instead of floating softly in the air, my arms went as stiff as broom handles, and I was sure I looked more like a mad windmill than a graceful ballerina.

I prayed for Miss Partridge to swap us over again, so I could return to the safety of the back row. But she didn't. Instead she began to set a new exercise –

one with *petits jetés*, *changements* and *assemblés* in it. As she showed us what she wanted, I was suddenly distracted by a strange whirring sound. Miss Partridge heard it too. She stopped what she was doing and said in a very respectful voice, 'Good afternoon, Madame.'

Everyone turned to follow her gaze. The studio door had opened and in came an old lady in an electric wheelchair. Her face was as wrinkled as tissue paper that's been screwed up and then smoothed out again. Above it her hair was a perfectly smooth cloud of white. You could have mistaken her for someone's kind granny – until you saw her eyes. They were blue, but it wasn't the soft blue of a spring sky or a pale flower. This blue was as bright and hot as the centre of a flame.

'Girls and boys,' Miss Partridge said to the class, 'I would like to introduce you to Madame Galina Evanova.'

A rustle of reaction swept through the room. Someone at the end of my row dropped a little curtsey, so I copied.

A gnarled hand flapped impatiently. 'Carry on, carry on,' said Galina Evanova.

'Yes, Madame.' And, after a moment's thought, Miss Partridge picked up where she had left off, marking out the exercise.

As the music began, I felt worse than ever. Galina Evanova – once a great ballerina and now the head of this famous school – was sitting just a metre or so away from me. My legs felt like jelly. Desperately I tried to jump as high as I could, to hold my arms well but not stiffly, to listen to the music . . . *and* get the steps right!

When the exercise was finished and the last notes of the piano died away, I saw with horror that Madame Evanova was whirring in my direction. She was about to say something. I held my position – feet in fifth, arms in a curve down in front of me, eyes staring straight ahead. Was it rude not to look at her? I didn't know if I dared.

She stopped right in front of me. Out of the corner of my eye I could see the elegant head tilt to one side. At last she spoke.

'You must stretch your knees harder. In the air – pah!' She shot her arm out before her, snapping the elbow straight so fast it made me jump. 'Think of the picture you create. Legs straight. Feet stretched. Make everything work harder – every cell in your body. And why do you look so serious? This is a ballet class – not a funeral.'

I waited for her to move on to the next person, like a general inspecting troops. But she didn't; she buzzed her wheelchair round on the spot, then, at a sedate pace, she proceeded towards the door. Mrs Seymour leapt up from behind the table to hold it open for her as she passed through.

I was still standing with my feet in fifth. But my chin was trembling. I felt utterly humiliated. To be the only one picked out for criticism in the whole class – that must mean I was the worst! And to be told off for something as babyish as not stretching my knees, too – Miss Cole would have been ashamed of me.

At that moment I knew, as certainly as if Madame had spoken the words herself: I would not get a place at the Evanova School.

Sixteen

I ran up the red-carpeted spiral staircase as fast as I could, clutching my character shoes to my chest, with echoes of the music Mrs Bates had played for our curtsies still ringing in my ears. I hadn't waited for Ella – I couldn't bear to.

As I flew along C corridor, the tears were already building up in my throat. Room 23 was empty – Luci wasn't back yet – and I slammed the door behind me and flung myself face down on my bed. I longed to be back at home with Mum and Dad and the twins; none of us need ever mention the name of this horrid, hateful school again.

There was a tap at the door. I sat up hurriedly, and wiped at my wet cheeks with the back of my hand.

'Hello?' I said, trying to make my voice sound light and normal.

The door opened a crack and Ella's dark eyes appeared. 'Oh, Sadie,' she said, hurrying in as she saw my tear-stained face. 'Are you OK?'

Her sympathetic expression set me off all over again, and I found myself snivelling into her shoulder as she sat beside me and gave me a hug.

'It's . . . hopeless . . .' I sobbed. 'I wish . . . I wish I'd never . . . come . . . here.'

'Don't say that.' Ella held me away from her and looked at me seriously. 'It's not necessarily a bad thing Madame picked you out, you know.'

'But I was the only one! She thought I was the worst of all–'

'Who says?' Ella looked at me straight. 'My teacher at home only bothers to be hard on pupils he thinks have a chance of being good. He leaves the bad ones alone because they're beyond help! I wouldn't mind betting Madame's just the same.'

I looked at her uncertainly.

'Honest,' she said. 'And I heard some of the girls on their way out of the studio saying they envied you being picked out like that.'

'You're just trying to make me feel better,' I said miserably. 'But thank you anyway,' I added, so as not to seem ungrateful.

Just then the door burst open. 'I'm back!' sang a loud voice.

Luci bounded through the door, then stopped abruptly. 'But what's happened here?' she said. 'Has disaster struck? Did you fall on your face? Or land in the pianist's lap?'

I had to smile. 'Nothing like that,' I said.

'Galina Evanova came into our class and singled Sadie out for correction,' explained Ella.

'She came into ours too,' said Pippa, who was right behind Luci. 'And I saw her watching me a lot.'

Luci ignored her. 'Was she fierce?' she said to me.

'Not really,' I admitted. 'I just . . . it's because I was so nervous, I suppose.'

'Well, all over now!' said Luci cheerily. 'It's impossible to tell what that lot thinks anyway. Don't worry – old Galina probably picked on you because she thought you were rather good.'

'Exactly what I said!' said Ella triumphantly.

'Well, why didn't she say anything to *me*, then?' inquired Pippa.

Luci rolled her eyes to the ceiling. Even Ella looked exasperated. '*Pippa*!' they both said together.

Pippa looked puzzled. 'What?' she said.

After supper that evening, there was a film showing in the Old Library: *Ondine*, a ballet by Sir Frederick Ashton, which he had choreographed especially for the world famous ballerina, Margot Fonteyn.

At seven thirty we all piled in. The Old Library was a beautiful room, with stained glass windows, and a great fireplace with a marble mantelpiece. At one end of the room they'd set up a big white projection screen, and in front of that were rows and rows of wooden chairs for us to sit on.

Luci, Ella, Pippa and I managed to get four seats together. Quite a few of the girls seemed to have made friends with each other now – and the boys were going around as one big group. Even Belinda, I noticed, was being trailed by a thin, pale girl who looked like she was listening to everything Belinda said with rapt attention.

The film is magical. It's the story of a water nymph, and Margot Fonteyn really makes you believe she isn't human at all, but some wonderful sprite. Her movements are so fluid and playful, and somehow she manages to make the steps look natural; it's as if she didn't even have to think about them – let alone rehearse for hours and hours to get them right.

When the lights went on afterwards, I felt like I'd been in the middle of a dream; I'd forgotten where I was, and, for a while at least, I'd even forgotten about the rotten audition.

Straight away, Pippa started telling us how her mother had danced Ondine countless times, and had been coached in the role by Margot Fonteyn herself. Luci looked annoyed, but I was fascinated. 'What was Margot Fonteyn like?' I asked.

'Very beautiful and gracious and kind,' said Pippa, with as much authority as if she had met her herself. 'Mummy thought she was the best dancer ever. Though I don't agree.'

'Who do you think was the best?' I asked.

'Why, Mummy of course,' said Pippa, clearly thinking it was a silly question. 'And I,' she added proudly, 'intend to be just as good.'

Luci scowled at this. I knew she thought Pippa was ever so big-headed. But I thought Pippa had every right to be proud – it *was* wonderful to have such a famous dancer as your mother, and I was certain Pippa must be a wonderful dancer too. She looked so regal – she walked like a princess, as if she was wearing a gown with a long train at the back. I suspect Luci was only pretending to be cross with her – deep down, she was probably as fascinated by Pippa as I was.

Seventeen

Brriinngg!

Seven a.m. I'd rather hoped we'd be allowed a Sunday lie-in, but no such luck. I stretched and yawned and looked across to Luci's bed on the other side of the room. She raised her rumpled head. 'Interviews with Miss Stretton this morning,' she said. 'Yeuch!'

It was the final test of the weekend. Every candidate was to have a one-to-one chat with the deputy headmistress. But, from what Luci had told me about Miss Stretton, I wasn't at all keen to meet her.

Her office was in a dark corner of one of the ground floor corridors, and by the time I'd sat in the gloom outside the door for ten minutes, waiting for the person before me to come out, I think I almost imagined I was about to meet a real-life dragon who would gobble me up in one gulp.

When I knocked on the door and went in, though, I just saw a bony woman in a dull green polo-neck jersey and a beige tweedy skirt. Her hair was slate grey, and swept back into a bun – not a tight knot high on her head like Miss Cole's, but a wide flat thing like a Danish pastry that nestled just where her hair stopped and her neck began. She had a cross little line between her eyebrows, which made it look as if she was always frowning, and thin, tight lips the colour of wallpaper paste.

'Sadie Marsh?' she said. I nodded.

'Please answer me verbally, child.' She looked at me severely. 'I cannot bear nervous little mice.'

Of course, that made me feel more like a mouse than ever, but I said 'Yes, Miss Stretton,' as confidently as I could, and sat down on the chair opposite her desk.

'You may sit,' she said pointedly, making it clear that I shouldn't have done so before.

She noted something on a sheet of paper in front of her – but I couldn't see what it was. A black mark for bad manners? I tried to tell myself it didn't matter; the audition had gone so badly I'd no chance of getting in anyway. What point was there in worrying what she thought of me?

Miss Stretton put down her pen, pressed the tips of her fingers together and looked at me over them. What would she ask me – the names of famous ballets? How many times I had been to the theatre? What an *entrechat* was? (I had heard Ella and Pippa talking about it earlier, but other than it being a jumping step I couldn't remember what they'd said.)

'You are a pupil at Middleton Combined School,' she said. 'Correct?'

'Yes, Miss Stretton.'

'And how do you find it?'

What a strange question, I thought. 'Well, if you

start at the town hall, go up the high street, turn left at the top–'

'No, no, no.' Miss Stretton gave a little sigh of exasperation. 'I am asking you what you think of it, not where it is.'

I blushed scarlet. Now she didn't just think me rude, she thought I was stupid as well.

The interview must have only lasted five or ten minutes, but it felt like an hour. When Miss Stretton asked what my favourite subjects were, I managed to get quite enthusiastic about long division, but then she cut me off, saying she had other candidates to see, and there were still more questions we had to get through. I didn't think that was terribly polite.

The she asked me why I wanted to come to the Evanova School and why I wanted to be a dancer. The first was easy: 'Because it's the best ballet school in the country, Miss Stretton,' I said.

But the second question was surprisingly difficult. It's hard to explain to somebody exactly why ballet is so wonderful, especially if they're fixing you with a really cold stare.

'It's the way the music takes you over . . . it – it feels really . . .' I hesitated, and Miss Stretton raised an eyebrow.

'I want to be like Moira Shearer in *The Red Shoes*,' I said at last.

'I see,' said Miss Stretton. I had the feeling it was the wrong answer.

All in all, I was glad when the interview was

over. And I wasn't the only one.

'That's it,' said Luci, arriving back from her interview some time later. 'I've really scuppered my chances now.'

'What did you do?' I asked, imagining her coming to blows with Miss Stretton and wrestling her to the floor.

'Oh, I told her I think some of the teachers at my school are far too strict and nasty,' said Luci breezily. 'Her eyes went narrow while I was talking. She doesn't approve of me at all.'

Once our interviews were over, we were allowed to do what we liked with the rest of the morning. It was a beautiful day – fresh and warm, with a gentle, rustling breeze – so Luci, Ella, Pippa and I decided to go and sit out in the school grounds. Beyond the lawns we found a wooded area and, following its path, we came to a little clearing shaded by the branches of a great beech tree. We decided to stop there.

'We will all keep in touch, won't we?' I asked, as Luci flopped down on her back, Ella sat and crossed her legs daintily in front of her, and Pippa patted the grass for dampness. 'I mean, I know the three of you will get in, so you'll see each other here, but if I write to you, will you write back?'

'I shan't get in, that's for certain,' said Luci, allowing only a hint of regret to creep into her voice. 'But Ella – I know they'll give you a place. You'll have to write and tell us what it's like.'

'Oh, I don't know about that,' said Ella, looking

down modestly. 'The getting in part, I mean. I'll definitely write.'

'I hate writing letters,' said Pippa, who'd settled herself at last on the grass and was looking at her feet as she pointed them in front of her. 'But, if Ella gets in too, I shall tell her what I think of it here, and she can put it in when she writes.' She leant back on her hands and looked up dreamily. 'I wonder which corridor my room will be on?'

I must admit I felt rather solemn at Sunday lunch. I met Belinda in the queue and agreed we should meet in the entrance hall at two o'clock ready to be picked up.

'How did your interview go?' I asked her.

'Oh – brilliantly,' she said breezily. She didn't ask about mine.

After lunch, Luci suggested we should all write down our addresses on little scraps of paper serviette and swap the pieces. I found out Luci and Pippa both lived in London – though somehow I didn't think they'd be arranging to see each other in a hurry – and Ella lived up in Edinburgh.

'I won't get home until very late tonight,' she said with a sigh. 'It's a good job it's the holidays and there's no school tomorrow.'

Then, inevitably, two o'clock came. The four of us fetched our bags from our rooms and waited together downstairs. Having chatted so easily all weekend, suddenly none of us seemed to be able to think of anything to say. Even so, I hoped Belinda's mother might be late, to give us as long as possible together. Unfortunately, though, she was one of the first to arrive.

It seemed bad to make a fuss of my new friends in front of Belinda, so I just said a quiet goodbye to Ella and Pippa. But then Luci grabbed me in a big hug before I had a chance to hesitate. 'So long, Sadie,' she said, and above the grin, her eyes looked a little watery. 'Keep in touch.'

Feeling watery myself, I nodded back and squeezed her hand.

Then Mrs Whitehead held the big wooden front door open and, with a last look back, I was gone.

Eighteen

I didn't feel like talking at all on the way home. Mrs Whitehead politely asked how my audition had gone, and I said, 'All right, thank you,' and nothing more. Perhaps it was a bit rude of me, but I don't think Mrs Whitehead was interested – what she really wanted to know about, of course, was Belinda's audition.

To my surprise, Belinda was acting like she'd been the belle of the ball all weekend.

'It was wonderful, Mummy! I made so many new friends – Laura, Annabel, Jessica . . .'

That was odd. Apart from that drippy-looking girl I'd seen Belinda with at the film-showing, I'd hardly seen her talking to anyone the whole weekend. I felt certain she couldn't be as confident about the audition as she was making out, either.

'It was pretty easy, really,' she said in an off-hand way. 'And the teacher said "Good" to me lots of times.'

I thought back to the audition, but I couldn't remember Miss Partridge praising Belinda once.

'. . . And in my interview, Miss Stretton said I showed great promise!'

'Wonderful, Belinda!' Mrs Whitehead turned and beamed at her proudly.

I had to look out of the window and bite my lip to stop myself laughing. I couldn't imagine Miss Stretton saying that to anyone, not even Lily Dempsey herself!

'I've brought your personal stereo,' said Mrs Whitehead over her shoulder when Belinda had finished her glowing description of the weekend. I saw it lying on the back seat between us. 'And I've brought two sets of headphones so you can both listen. I think the tape that's in is the music for *La Fille Mal Gardée*, isn't it darling?'

Belinda checked. 'That's right, Mummy,' she said brightly, and pushed the spare set of headphones towards me.

But when I put the headphones on, I found Belinda wouldn't let me plug them into the stereo. I went to take them off again, but she motioned at me angrily not to. She didn't want me to listen, but didn't want her mother to know either.

It wasn't worth arguing. So I spent the whole journey with the headphones clamped on my ears, listening to nothing.

Nineteen

'This cupboard,' said Mrs Winter, pointing accusingly at it as if somehow its messiness were its own fault, 'needs a thorough clearing out. *Thorough.*'

So, with a wicker wastepaper basket in one hand, and a voluminous yellow duster in the other, I set to work.

It was a Sunday morning, three weeks after the audition. It hadn't been a very happy three weeks.

After Mrs Whitehead had dropped me home from the audition I'd discovered a hole in my coat pocket. It was the pocket I'd put the precious scraps of serviette in, and two of them had fallen out. The only one left was Luci's. I wrote to Luci the next day – a long letter, with a drawing of my bedroom and the front of my house in it. I asked her to send me Ella and Pippa's addresses too. But I never heard back. The one good thing about the audition – the friends I'd made – seemed as if it had disappeared.

So for three weeks I'd felt flat and miserable. I'd even wondered whether it was worth starting the summer term with Miss Cole. If I wasn't good enough to get into the Evanova, I wasn't good enough to be a dancer, so why waste my time going to classes?

But in the end I couldn't bear the thought of no ballet. I *did* start the new term with Miss Cole – and

I carried on helping Mrs Winter on Sundays to pay for it, too.

The cupboard she'd set me to work on this particular morning was in one corner of her drawing-room. It was made of thick, dark wood, and the doors had fake twisting columns at the outer edges, which made the whole thing look grander than it was.

Inside, mess bulged from every shelf and drawer. As soon as I tugged on one thing, an avalanche began, and the next moment the floor around me was ankle-deep in old cardboard files, photo albums and bundles of yellow-edged letters tied together with pieces of string.

'I've never been able to throw anything away!' declared Mrs Winter proudly when she came in and saw the chaos. 'My life – my whole past – is in that cupboard.'

The idea of Mrs Winter having a past at all seemed strange. I couldn't imagine her any other way than how she was now – with her wrinkled face, her saggy brown dresses and her glorious hats.

When I'd sorted the mess into orderly piles on the carpet, I picked up one of the photo albums and opened it. The pages were made of thick black card, and the photographs seemed thick too – like little table mats. Most of them had the name of a photographer stamped in flourishing, curly letters in one corner.

The first few photos were of stern-looking elderly ladies in lace caps and black dresses, and some gentlemen too, with stiff high collars on their shirts. Then there were several children, in sailor suits and best Sunday dresses, standing in solemn poses like miniature versions of their parents and grandparents.

But when I turned the last page I saw a quite different photograph. It was of two teenage girls. They were dressed identically – as ballerinas. They wore light, loose-sleeved blouses under tight little bodices, and skirts that fanned out into heavy-looking tutus. On their feet were satin ballet shoes that looked much softer than the ones the assistant in Dancewear had shown me, yet one of the girls was balancing on pointe, with her leg raised in the *attitude* position in front of her. Her hand rested lightly on the shoulder of her companion for support.

'Found something?' said Mrs Winter behind me. I jumped. I hadn't even realised she was in the room.

'I-I'm sorry,' I stammered, hastily closing the album. 'I was just–'

'Stop fretting, my dear!' she commanded. 'I don't mind in the slightest. In fact, if I hadn't completely forgotten it was there, I might have shown you that photograph myself.'

Tentatively, I opened the album again, and turned back to the photograph of the two girls.

'Who were they?' I asked.

'Well,' Mrs Winter bent down and tapped the nail of her index finger on one of the faces. 'That, my dear, was a girl called Gail Evans.' She turned her eyes to me, as if expecting some reaction. I looked blank.

'Soon after this was taken,' said Mrs Winter, 'she adopted a stage name. The fashion then was for all ballet dancers to be Russian, of course, so she chose a name that sounded appropriate. Galina Evanova.'

I gasped, and looked back at the photograph. I held it up close to my face, searching for some resemblance between this smooth-skinned young girl and the elderly lady I had seen at the audition. Yes, there was the same high forehead, the same firm set of the mouth. The face looked softer, though, and gentler.

I sighed. 'Wow. *The* Galina Evanova.'

Mrs Winter grunted. She was very particular about words she liked and didn't like. 'Wow' was one she didn't. But for once, she said nothing.

'And who was the other girl?' I asked, holding the album out for her to see again.

'That,' said Mrs Winter simply, 'was me.'

I sipped my lemonade and savoured the sharpness washing over my tongue. For once, Mrs Winter had served our eleven o'clock drinks half an hour early – I looked in need of them, she'd said. I think it was the shock.

'You assumed I'd always been a piano teacher, I suppose?' said Mrs Winter, settling back in her chair on the opposite side of the fireplace to mine.

I nodded. Always old, always a piano teacher . . . though, now I came to think of it, I *had* at first wondered how she knew so much about ballet.

Mrs Winter adjusted her hat – it was a close-fitting one; she called it a 'cloche' – and leant her head back, with a misty look in her eyes I'd seen once before.

'We were inseparable, Gail and I,' she said. 'At that time, being a dancer wasn't thought respectable by some people, you see. Both our fathers were very against it – and it made us stick together. We ran away to Paris when we were fourteen to join the great Strahov's company. Gail became one of his favourite "baby ballerinas". That was how her fame began.'

'And you?' I asked. I felt as if I was looking at Mrs Winter for the first time. Why had I never noticed before how elegantly she held her head, how slender she was, how graceful, despite her aches and pains?

'Me? Oh, I was never a great dancer. A good one . . . perhaps even very good – it is not for me to say. But never great. Not like Gail. So when I had an offer of marriage from a gentle, kind man – a man who asked me, if I was to accept him, to give up my career on the stage – I felt that I had to do as he said.'

'You gave up ballet?' I asked, scarcely able to imagine how a dancer could make such an awful choice.

'What else could I do?' Mrs Winter looked at me suddenly. 'I was never going to become as famous as Gail. And dancing is such a young person's profession – an old lady can earn money as a piano teacher, but not as a dancer.' She smiled. 'In those days, marriage meant security. And security was something I needed.

I thought about teaching ballet, naturally –' she paused again as she sipped her drink '– but there was already a dancing mistress who held her classes near where we lived. There was, though, no one to teach piano.'

'And did you keep in touch with Galina . . . Gail, I mean?' I asked.

Here a glimmer of amusement lit up Mrs Winter's face. 'Why yes,' she said, and waved her hand towards the sideboard. A small reproduction of a painting was propped against a vase. 'I received that card from her just last week.'

For the second time that morning, my mouth dropped open in shock. 'But . . .' I thought about it for a moment. 'No wonder you knew so much about the Evanova School!'

'Quite!' said Mrs Winter. 'Did you think I made it up? Or that it was just part of an old lady's general knowledge?'

I blushed, and looked down at my lemonade. 'I . . . I don't know.'

'Well, don't worry, my dear. I consider your faith in me a great compliment,' said Mrs Winter, with a smile. Then she saw my expression change. A thought had just occurred to me, and Mrs Winter guessed what it was. 'No, Sadie,' she said gently. 'I haven't asked Gail about your audition. It would not have been proper for me to do so.'

'Of course,' I said. These amazing discoveries about Mrs Winter had suddenly made a fresh wave of hope rise up in me. The hope that somehow, despite everything, I still had a chance of following in her footsteps. It was a silly thought. I shook my head to get rid of it.

'No – *don't* give up hope,' said Mrs Winter, reading my expression. 'If you are determined to succeed, and have the talent to do it, you will always find a way.'

'But what if I don't have the talent?' I said, looking at her desperately.

'*I* believe,' said Mrs Winter, sitting up very straight and pulling her hat down over her ears, '*I* believe, my dear, that you *do*.'

Part Three

The Dream

Twenty

The next day – at last – I got a letter from Luci.

'Hi there, Sadie,' she'd written. 'How's it going? Summer in London is going to be great – I just wish you lived nearer so we could do things together . . .'

She'd forgotten to send me the other addresses, but she had drawn a picture of her bedroom for me, and the front of her block of flats, too. 'And this is our new puppy,' she wrote, beside a drawing of something with four legs and two very long, floppy ears. 'He's causing chaos and driving Mum up the wall even more than I do (and that's saying something!). We've called him Rocket.'

Then she got on to the subject of the audition. 'I'm getting to feel almost glad I won't get in to the Evanova,' she wrote. 'Because Frankie – that's my little sister – said she'd cry every night if I went away. Now she tells me! Usually she's on at me like she hates my guts. Kids, eh?'

I smiled to myself at that. I missed Luci. And,

despite what she said, I didn't share her doubts about the audition. There was such enthusiasm in her for everything. I could just imagine how lively and dazzling her dancing would be. I was sure she'd get in.

I had no doubts about the other two, either. Ella looked like a born dancer – and when I'd glimpsed her in our audition, she'd seemed every bit as good as I'd expected. She had a natural grace, and very neat footwork, especially in her jumps.

And Pippa? She was the daughter of Clara Parnell, after all – how could she possibly fail?

No. I was sure I'd be the only one left behind. Just like the little boy in the Pied Piper story.

'I'm home!' After school that afternoon I slammed through the door as usual, and dumped my satchel and coat by the pegs in the little narrow hallway.

'Hello, love.' Mum was in the kitchen. It was Friday, but for once she wasn't at the old people's home. Dad had been away for three days lecturing in London, though he was due back tonight, and Tina was on holiday, so she'd had to miss her visit.

'How was school?'

'Oh, Mr Rodgers got cross with us about decimals again and Darren Plaistow hit Rebecca Brown and tried to put ketchup in her hair.'

'That's nice.' Mum hadn't been listening. 'We had some post today.'

She reached over to the post rack and handed me

a white envelope. In one corner was the Evanova School crest: a shield with a pair of ballet shoes on it, their long ribbons dangling down, and the two masks of drama on either side – one happy, one sad.

The envelope was addressed to 'Dr and Mrs Marsh', but Mum said, 'I thought you might like to open it yourself.'

All at once my heartbeat seemed to be throbbing in my ears. I put my thumb under the corner of the envelope flap and waggled it up and down, making ragged tears all along the top. Inside, the paper was folded with razor-sharp creases. My hand shook as I drew it out, unfolded it, and turned it the right way up.

'Dear Dr and Mrs Marsh . . .' The words swam before my eyes.

'Well?' Mum looked at me anxiously, trying to see the letter's news reflected in my expression.

'Oh, Mum!' Suddenly my face crumpled.

'Never mind, Sadie, never mind.' She put her arms round me and stroked my hair comfortingly. 'Rotten school anyway, eh?'

'But Mum,' I emerged from her grasp and managed a watery smile. 'I've got in!'

Twenty-one

Mum did say well done of course – several times. But the next thing she said was, 'A scholarship. Sadie – did you get a scholarship?'

I'd forgotten all about that. Hurriedly I looked at the letter again. It didn't mention anything about it. And then I saw there was a second sheet of paper behind the first, with 'Scholarship Update' written across the top.

' "Because of an unexpected and unavoidable withdrawal of funds by one of our benefactors . . ." ' Mum was reading out loud, with a worried expression on her face. ' " . . .we regret to say that no scholarships can be offered to new Evanova pupils this year." ' She lowered her hands and looked at me. 'Oh, Sadie–'

'No!' I cried suddenly. 'Mum, *no*! Don't say we can't afford it, *don't*! I'll find the money. I'll sell things – my clothes, my books, everything! Please – Mum!'

'This is all Simon's fault,' Mum said bitterly, shaking her head. 'With his silly, one-step-at-a-time attitude. We should never have let you audition in the first place . . .'

It was more than I could bear. When, a minute later, the door banged and Dad's voice announced loudly, 'I'm home! Your wonderful, clever Dad is home!' his jolly tone was met with wails from me and a thunderous scowl from Mum.

But Dad heard the whole story with a broad grin on his face. 'Well done, Tiger!' he said, and whirled me round in a big hug. I clung to the shoulder of his shirt. It soon got rather soggy.

'Simon!' Mum looked really angry. 'See the misery you've caused her! How can you be so happy when there's no way we can pay for her to go to this school!'

Dad set me down, and looked at Mum with shining eyes. 'Oh, but we can,' he said quietly.

I looked up. 'Jill.' Solemnly Dad went down on one knee in front of Mum. 'Please forgive me. I told an untruth.'

Mum's anger changed to confusion. 'What about?'

'I said I was lecturing in London for three days,' said Dad. 'Well – I wasn't. I'm afraid that I was doing something else instead. I was being a contestant on *The Golden Ticket*.'

Mum opened her mouth to speak, but Dad held up a hand. 'They filmed my round, the quarter finals, the semis and the final all in three days. And what happened, you see,' the big grin crept back on to his face, 'what happened was that yours truly – Simon Marsh – the cleverest Dad in the world . . . won! The whole thing!' Mum looked at him like he'd flipped completely. Dad didn't seem to care. He carried on, 'And the money I won will cover Sadie's fees for the first year – and buy us a really nice holiday besides!'

Well, you can imagine – it was mayhem in our

house after that. Dad had to explain everything all over again and show Mum the cheque for his winnings, before she'd believe him. But when she did she laughed and clapped and hugged him and hugged me, and promised never to say quiz shows were a waste of time again.

Dad, meanwhile, skipped about the kitchen like a mad grey-haired leprechaun, whirling me round and round till I was hopelessly dizzy. Then he went into the sitting-room to whirl the twins round too. This gave the twins such uncontrollable fits of giggles that they were both sick, which calmed Dad down a bit, as Mum made him clear it up.

'Sadie, you must ring Miss Cole to tell her,' said Mum.

'May I ring Mrs Winter, too?' I asked. Mum nodded.

I really wanted to tell Mrs Winter, but I was nervous about it, as I hadn't ever rung her at home before and I thought she might be cross at being disturbed. But she wasn't cross – and when she said, 'Oh very well done, my dear – I'm proud of you!' I could hear the smile in her voice, and I felt so thrilled I thought I'd burst.

When I finally got to bed, I felt so happy I thought I would float above the duvet all night.

The next morning I could hardly believe it was still true.

At breakfast, though, I had a horrible thought. What if they'd got the lists mixed up and they hadn't meant to accept me at all – or the names mixed up and they thought I was someone else?

'Please, Mum,' I begged. 'Will you ring the school to check?'

'Don't be silly.' She smiled. 'You just worry too much.'

So I tried Dad instead.

'Please, please, please, Dad! Pretty please! I won't sleep all summer if you don't!'

Dad laughed. 'Oh well, I'd better ring then, hadn't I?'

He dialled the number and got Miss Featherstone (who was in her office, even on a Saturday).

'Good morning,' I heard him say politely. 'Could I just ask you to check – to double-triple-quadruple check in fact . . .'

'Dad!' I hissed at him. He could be so embarrassing sometimes!

' . . . And you do know,' he went on, 'that Sadie Marsh is the little girl with the long brown hair and the pale skin like a glass of milk, don't you? Yes – yes, of course. I just wanted to be sure you had the right person. Thank you, Miss Featherstone.'

'Well!' Dad put down the receiver. 'We *do* know what we are doing, *thank* you Dr Marsh, and we are *not* in the habit of sending the *wrong* letters to the *wrong* people at *any* time, let *alone* on such an important matter . . .'

I giggled with delight – he sounded just like her!

All this while, of course, I was busy wondering what

had happened to Luci and Ella and Pippa – I was so hoping they'd got in too!

I scribbled a letter to Luci before ballet, but I ran out of time, so I had to leave Ella's and Pippa's until later. Then, when I got to the community centre, I ran straight up to Belinda in the waiting room. For once Mrs Whitehead wasn't with her.

'Did you get a letter?' I asked breathlessly.

She looked at me coldly. 'It's a stupid school, you know,' she said. 'Certainly not as good as it used to be, Mummy says. The Hampton is much better these days. I'm going to try for it next year. We've sent off for a brochure this morning.'

I didn't need to ask what Belinda's letter had said. She didn't ask me about mine, and I hadn't the heart to tell her I'd got in. I don't think it had ever occurred to her that I might.

Twenty-two

Why did Luci never write back to me? All over the summer I couldn't puzzle it out. I knew that she was slow at writing letters, but I thought the news of whether or not we'd got into the Evanova would make her pick up her pen.

I wasn't surprised that I didn't hear from Pippa, though. She'd said how much she hated writing. Besides, I was pretty certain she'd got a place.

The one letter I did get was from Ella.

'I'm in too!' she wrote. 'I can't quite believe it . . . and I can't wait to see you again. It's going to be brilliant . . .'

I knew it was – but I still found myself worrying about Luci. I wanted to write to her again, but I didn't dare. Perhaps she hadn't got a place after all, and was feeling really miserable? As the weeks went by and no letter arrived, I knew that was what must have happened. And though I was still excited about going to the Evanova, I had to admit it seemed a much lonelier prospect without her.

Then the school holidays came and with Dad's winnings we went on a brilliant trip to Scotland. When we got back, there was a big parcel waiting for me. It was my new uniform – for school and for dancing. They'd kept all my measurements from the medical and allowed a bit of 'growing into' room, which Mum was grateful for. I tried the school uniform on: the dark blue skirt, the white blouse, and the blue and white striped blazer, with the school crest on the pocket. It felt like the best outfit in the world.

I went round to show Mrs Winter.

'I am pleased Gail still insists on hats,' she said, examining the felt winter hat and the summer straw boater, which had a crown so hard and flat it was like wearing a teatray on your head. 'So many schools these days have dispensed with headgear, and in my view it is a sorry waste. One must learn to wear hats well –' she planted the boater on my head, at a rakish angle I knew Miss Stretton would disapprove of '– and how is one to learn if one can never practise, hm? A whole generation will grow up having never worn hats and the art will be lost, quite lost.'

In what seemed like no time at all, it was the final week of the holidays. I'd had my last lesson with Miss Cole the Saturday before and she'd announced in front of the whole class that I would be going to the Evanova. A gasp had gone round the room, and even Julian, the troublemaker, had looked at me enviously. Mr Arthur had flashed me a special smile over the piano lid, too. But down in the front row Belinda had burst into tears, and run out of the room so fast that the swing doors thudded back and forth for ages afterwards. Miss Cole didn't say anything and just carried on with the class. And when it'd ended and I got outside, Belinda had already gone.

For my final piano lesson Mrs Winter wore an extra special hat – one I hadn't seen before. It was dark blue with a large curved feather that stuck up like a question mark. We hardly did any work; I'd only played a couple of pieces when she told me to sit in the armchair while she went to the kitchen.

To my surprise, instead of just bringing two glasses of her special lemonade, Mrs Winter produced a big tea – 'high tea' she called it – with tiny egg and cress sandwiches with the crusts cut off, and little fairy cakes she'd made herself. (Her hand had slipped, she said, when she'd put the food colouring in the icing, so it was shocking pink!)

'A fine send-off,' said Mrs Winter. I was too busy trying to stop the egg spurting out of my sandwich to reply.

After we'd finished eating, Mrs Winter smoothed down her skirt with her thin hands and announced, 'I have a present for you, my dear. Go into my closet –' this was the guest bedroom upstairs, but Mrs Winter called it her closet '– to the second cupboard from the left under the window. Bring what you find there.'

I hurried upstairs, and found the cupboard. There was nothing in it, except for a cardboard box, sealed with thick brown sticky tape. It didn't look much like a present, but nevertheless I carefully slid my fingers round the bottom corners and pulled it out. It was quite heavy. I tapped the cupboard door shut with quite heavy. I tapped the cupboard door shut with my foot, and went back downstairs.

'Don't give it to me,' said Mrs Winter as I came back into the drawing-room and approached her chair. 'It is for you.'

I sat down and put the box on my lap. The brown tape was extremely sticky, and it took me quite a while to peel all the pieces off – but the best thing about a parcel is opening it, I always think, so I didn't mind that it took so long.

At last I pulled the top flaps of cardboard apart and looked inside. There was an oblong of shiny black, surrounded by cotton-wool. I pulled the black thing out.

'Oh – Mrs Winter, it's beautiful!' I exclaimed, holding it up in front of me, and turning it this way and that so I could see every side.

'It's very old,' said Mrs Winter. 'You must take extra special care of it.'

It was a black wooden box, divided into two sections. On the right-hand side the top of the box formed a lid, fastened with a little clasp. Below the lid there were several drawers edged in delicate pink and yellow paint. On the left-hand side was a glass panel, and through it I could see a tiny dancer, dressed in a long white floaty skirt. The dancer looked like she was made of some sort of metal, like an old toy soldier, and her face and hair were very carefully painted on, though there was a little scratch on the very tip of her nose. Behind her, there was a small mirror, and I could see that tiny net wings sprouted from the back of her dress, which was made of real fabric.

'Open the lid,' Mrs Winter instructed me.

I undid the golden clasp and pushed the lid up. As I did so, a soft tinkling tune began to play, and the little dancer, behind her glass window, started to turn around.

'It's a theme from *Swan Lake,*' said Mrs Winter. 'Which is rather strange – since the dancer looks like she is dressed for *Les Sylphides.*'

'Is it really a present for me?' I asked. I couldn't believe she could bear to part with something so beautiful.

'It is for you to safeguard, yes,' she said. 'But I must tell you – it is not yours to own, any more than it is mine to give.'

'What do you mean?' I looked at Mrs Winter.

'The dancer who gave it to me in Paris a long time ago told me it must be passed from dancer to dancer as the years go by,' she explained. 'It had been given to her by a dancer at the Imperial Russian court, and when she gave it to me, she said that I too should pass it on some day. Perhaps I should not have kept it for so long, but I have never found the right person to be its next owner – until now.'

'I shall take very good care of it,' I promised, carefully fitting it back into its box. 'And one day, I shall pass it on to someone – I shan't forget.'

Mrs Winter nodded, satisfied. Then she reached

down beside her feet and produced, with a flourish, the butterscotch tin. 'High time we delved in here, my dear, don't you think?'

Twenty-three

'See the sea, see the sea,' Oliver chanted.

'No, you can't,' said Mum patiently. 'We're an awfully long way from the sea, Oliver. You'll have to make do with trees and fields instead.'

The day had come at last, and we were speeding along in the car on the way to the Evanova School. All my luggage for a whole term was in two big cases in the boot. I kept worrying that I'd forgotten something vital, like my pyjamas, or Mrs Winter's precious music box or–

'Don't look so worried, Tiger!' said Dad, glancing at me over his shoulder.

'Keep your eyes on that route, Simon,' said Mum, who was driving. Dad was in charge of the map, but Mum said she didn't trust him to find his way out of a paper bag, never mind get us all the way to the Evanova – even though he *had* been there once before. Dad turned back guiltily to study the road signs.

My stomach felt very churny, and every time we stopped I had to get out and find a loo. I was excited, but dreading it too and, most of all, dreading the horrible moment when I would have to say goodbye to Mum, Dad and the twins.

I didn't want the journey to end. But when I

spotted the red-brick tower peeping up over the treetops, a thrill ran through me. Dad said suddenly, 'Turn here, turn here!' and, just in time, Mum managed to lurch the car into the driveway.

'I think we can go through the arch and park in the centre courtyard,' said Dad. I wondered if he was remembering, as I was, how the gates had been shut and padlocked last time he'd been here.

'My, isn't it posh!' said Mum. 'Our daughter's going to live in a castle!'

I lugged one of my cases up to the big wooden door. Mum and Dad followed with the other case, and one twin each. Thomas and Oliver were sucking their thumbs and craning their heads round to look at the strange building.

Stepping into the hallway, we came upon Miss Featherstone, brandishing her clipboard. 'That's the one you talked to on the phone,' I whispered to Dad.

'Sadie *Marsh*, isn't it?' said Miss Featherstone, coming forward to peer at me. When I nodded, she made a mark on her list, then turned to two older pupils who were waiting beside her, smart in their blue and white striped blazers.

'Jenna MacGregor,' she said to one of them, 'this is Sadie Marsh. She has been allocated C15.' She turned back to me. 'Jenna MacGregor will take you to your room,' she said.

Dad picked up one of my cases, but Miss Featherstone waggled a finger at him. 'I'm sure Jenna and Sadie can manage those, *thank* you, Dr Marsh. We might as well get the goodbyes over *quickly*, yes?' With that, she turned away to another set of parents who had just come in.

Jenna stepped forward and smiled. She looked very friendly – and faintly familiar, though I couldn't think why.

I turned to Mum and Dad, and suddenly there was a lump in my throat.

'Well, Tiger,' said Dad, ruffling my hair. 'You be a good girl and take care.'

'We'll write as often as we can,' added Mum, and they both enveloped me in a big hug, with the twins squashed in as well. I kissed everyone in turn, and the twins – sensing something they didn't quite understand – began to grizzle.

'We'd better put these two in the car before they really get going,' said Mum. So, with a last wave, they turned towards the door, and I turned the other way to follow Jenna. I looked back just before we rounded the corner, but they had already gone.

Hurrying after Jenna along the corridor, I saw we were heading for the spiral staircase I remembered so well.

'Can you manage that?' Jenna asked, nodding towards the case I was carrying. It was the lighter of the two, but it was still pretty weighty.

'Oh . . . yes,' I puffed. 'Thank you.'

She smiled, and I was dazzled. She looked like a real dancer, even in her ordinary school uniform.

And that face was so familiar – where could I possibly have seen her before?

On the first floor, Jenna swung open the heavy fire door that marked the beginning of C corridor and stood back to let me through. All at once, memories of the audition weekend came flooding back. I wished Luci was here – I would never be lonely or homesick with her around. As we came to a halt in front of a door marked C15, not too far from the room Luci and I had shared, I could almost hear that Australian voice. 'Jeepers! I've only gone and forgotten my toothbrush!'

Jenna smiled as she reached for the doorknob. 'Sounds like your roommate's here already.'

I was startled. She'd heard the voice too? Did that mean . . . ? I burst into the room.

'My goodness, Sadie!' said Luci, laughing. 'What an entrance! But then you always did go for dramatic ones I guess!' We hugged one another tightly. Jenna looked on in amusement.

'No introductions needed, I think,' she said, setting down my case. 'I'll leave you to it.'

As she turned to go, I suddenly realised where I had seen her face before. 'Jenna?' I said. She stopped and faced me again. 'That photo on the front of the school brochure – is it you?'

Jenna looked surprised for a moment, then laughed. 'Yes! I'm the little one at the front. How clever of you to recognise me – it was taken three years ago, and I thought I'd changed quite a bit.'

I was about to tell her how many hours I'd spent staring at her photo and wishing I could be just like her – but then I realised how silly it would sound.

'See you later, then,' she said, as she went back into the corridor.

'Thanks, Jenna!' I called after her. Then I turned to Luci – I had another important question. 'Why on earth didn't you tell me you'd got in? You never replied to my letter!'

'I did too!' Luci protested. 'The very day I got it! I listed all my theories on why they'd given me a place. Miss Stretton having a brainstorm was my favourite.'

'Well, it never arrived,' I said.

'Weird.' Luci thought for a moment. 'Unless . . . Now, hang on . . . Mum said something about Rocket chewing up some paper. She couldn't tell but she thought it might have been a letter. It never occurred to me that it was mine – but I bet it was! I gave it to my step-dad to post and he must have left it somewhere–'

'Never mind now,' I said, laughing at her worried expression. 'I think it was worth it – seeing you here without expecting to was the best surprise I've ever had!'

Luci looked really pleased at that, but she didn't have time to say anything as there was a knock on the door.

'May I come in?'

Luci and I looked at each other. 'Ella!' we cried in unison. The minute she was through the door we grabbed her in a double hug so tight she had to get her breath back.

'I can't believe we're together again!' she said at last, her eyes shining.

'Are you on this corridor?' asked Luci.

Ella nodded. 'Three doors along. But I'm not sure who I'm sharing with.'

And that's when we heard another voice.

'Do you mean I haven't been given a room to myself *again*?' it asked imperiously.

We all looked at one another and burst out giggling. Ella ran to the door. 'Pippa! Pippa!' she called. 'We're in here!'